Pumpkin Pie & Piercing Hearts

By

Tanisha Pollard

Pumpkin Pie & Piercing Hearts

ISBN: 979-8-9935159-0-8 (Paperback)

ISBN: 979-8-9935159-1-5 (Ebook)

Tanisha Pollard

First Edition: 2025

Published by: Self-Published

Cover design: Olivia

Interior formatting: Tanisha Pollard

Dedication

For anyone who's ever stolen a look across the counter, argued over flour, and ended up kissing someone you swore you shouldn't.

For every messy kitchen, every slow burn, and every pie that tasted like love.

This one's for the rivals who became lovers, the hearts that couldn't stay away, and the stories that leave you hungry for more.

Tanisha Pollard

Table of Contents

Pumpkin Pie & Piercing Hearts

Tanisha Pollard

Prologue

The crisp autumn air carried the scent of cinnamon and roasted pumpkin, curling around the streets of Maplewood like a warm, inviting hug. Emma Lawson pulled her knitted scarf tighter, ignoring the flurry of leaves that danced at her ankles, and fumbled with the wicker basket of fresh apples she had just picked from Mrs. Miller's orchard.

It was the week before the annual Thanksgiving Pie Festival, the event that had both made and broken local bakers' reputations for generations. Emma loved the festival, not just for the competition, but for the way the town transformed into a canvas of gold, amber, and rust. The perfect backdrop for her favorite part of the year: baking.

Her basket nearly tipped when someone's voice cut through the bustling crowd.

"Emma Lawson?"

She froze, scanning the market. Her heart betrayed her, skipping a beat for a reason she shouldn't feel after all these years. There he was—Noah Carter—hands in the pockets of his leather jacket, a crooked smile tugging at his lips. The same stormy blue eyes she had once thought were hers to admire from afar in high school.

"You still make that pumpkin pie everyone raves about?" he asked, tilting his head.

Emma's hands tightened on the basket. "And you still know how to ruin a perfectly good morning?" she shot back, tone sharper than she intended.

A chuckle escaped him, low and familiar. "Some things never change."

She wanted to glare, wanted to shove him into the nearest pile of hay, but all she could do was notice the way his presence made her chest tighten in a way she had not expected. After all these years, the sparks of teenage crushes didn't always burn out—they sometimes smoldered quietly, waiting for the perfect moment to flare.

And maybe, just maybe, this Thanksgiving would be that moment.

Chapter 1

Pumpkin Spice & Dreams

The scent of cinnamon and brown sugar filled the air long before sunrise. Emma Lawson moved through the bakery like clockwork—sleeves rolled, curls pinned up, heart steady. The ovens hummed behind her, the same rhythm that had filled this kitchen since her grandmother's time.

Morning light caught the framed photo by the register: Grandma Mae, pearls and apron in place, smiling like she could see straight through Emma's excuses. The honey-colored walls glowed against Emma's caramel skin, flour dusting her brown curls like snow that didn't belong but stayed, anyway.

Her grandmother used to hum gospel songs while kneading dough, swaying her hips just a little. *"You can't rush love or crust, baby. Both need time to rise."*
 Emma still heard her voice when the world went quiet.

The bell above the door jingled as sunlight spilled across polished counters and rows of pumpkin pies cooling on the rack. It should have felt like home—her dream, her legacy—but lately, even nutmeg couldn't fill the silence that lingered after closing.

She brushed flour from her apron and glanced at the contest flyer taped to the counter:
MAPLEWOOD'S ANNUAL THANKSGIVING BAKE-OFF
Winner's pie featured statewide.

It was the kind of opportunity Grandma Mae would've pushed her toward. A way to prove that Lawson Bakery—Black-owned and woman-built—belonged right there with the best of them. A way to show she'd made something out of all that grief and grit.

"Grandma," she whispered to the empty room, "I hope I make you proud."

The ovens beeped. Outside, Maplewood was waking up—church bells, delivery trucks, the familiar pulse of small-town life. Emma tied her apron tighter, trying to ignore the flicker of nerves that came with wanting more.

Just as she reached for a cooling rack, the door jingled again.

Hazel Grant breezed in, a burst of orange scarf, laughter, and attitude. Her warm brown skin glowed against the morning light, and her curls were pulled up in a bun that looked like it had survived a windstorm—and won.

"Please tell me you're entering that bake-off," Hazel said, leaning across the counter to sniff a pie. "Because if you don't, I will. And you know mine would taste like regret and undercooked ambition."

Emma laughed, shaking her head. "You burn toast, Hazel."

"Exactly," Hazel said, grinning. "That's why I'm depending on you. Besides, the whole town's talking about the competition this year."

Emma reached for a towel, wiping down the counter. "Let them talk."

Hazel's grin widened. "Oh, I'm talking. Especially since I heard **he's back**."

Emma's hand stilled. "He?"

Hazel tilted her head, teasing. "Don't play innocent. The diner's reopening next week. Guess who's running it now?"

Emma's chest tightened, the air thickening like syrup. "Noah Carter?"

Hazel's eyes gleamed. "Mmhmm. The same one. Fresh haircut, new attitude. Apparently, he's entering the contest too."

Emma forced a steady breath, pretending to check the ovens. "Good for him."

"Good for him," Hazel repeated with a laugh. "Not so good for you though, huh?"

Emma shot her a look that could curdle milk. "Hazel, I have pies to finish."

Hazel raised her hands, backing toward the door. "Fine, fine. Just don't burn anything while you're brooding over your ex-almost-something."

When the door closed behind her, Emma turned back to the flyer, her reflection wavering in the glass.

The contest had been about legacy before.
Now it was something else entirely.

Chapter 2

The One That Got Away

The bell above the diner door jingled, that same nostalgic chime that used to ring through Emma's childhood weekends — back when her father would take her for pancakes after Sunday service.
Only now, the place had changed.

The booths were reupholstered in warm caramel leather. New copper lights hung above the counter, glinting off the glass sugar jars. The scent of butter, coffee, and sizzling bacon filled the air — familiar and yet, different.

Emma hesitated just inside the doorway, her tray of pumpkin pie samples trembling slightly in her hands. She *knew* who owned the place now — Hazel had told her. Told her *gleefully*, in fact.

"Go on," Hazel had said that morning, eyes glinting. "You'll want to see how he's running it now. Maybe even how *he's* looking now."

Emma had rolled her eyes at the time, pretending she didn't care. Pretending she wasn't curious.
But as her gaze swept the diner and landed on him

— on *Noah Carter* — that fragile wall of indifference cracked instantly.

Behind the counter, in a crisp white button-down and black slacks, sleeves rolled to the elbow, Noah moved with easy confidence. His brown skin caught the morning light, his dark hair slightly mussed, and that smile — soft, knowing, too damn sure of itself — made her heartbeat trip.

He looked older, steadier, maybe a little more tired. But those gray-blue eyes hadn't changed at all.

"Noah Carter," she said under her breath, almost like a curse.

He turned then — and when their eyes met, the years between them vanished.

"Emma Lawson," he said softly, a grin spreading slow and sure. "Still showing up wherever the best pie is."

She raised an eyebrow, steadying her grip on the tray. "You mean *my* pie."

His laugh was low and familiar, curling in her stomach like old memories. "Guess we'll see about that at the contest."

Emma set the tray on the counter, ignoring how her pulse jumped. "So it's true. You actually own the place now."

"Yeah." His gaze softened as he glanced around. "It was my Aunt Celeste's. She left it to me when she passed last year. I wasn't sure if I could handle it, but... the diner didn't feel right without family in it."

Her chest tightened. Everyone in Maplewood had loved Celeste — the woman with the easy laugh and extra biscuits for every kid. "I didn't know she passed."

"Yeah," he said quietly. "Cancer. Quick and cruel. But she taught me everything about running this place. I couldn't just let it go."

Emma nodded, something like sympathy flashing through her irritation. "So you came back."

He looked at her for a long moment. "Guess I did."

"You could've written," she said finally. "Or called. You know, like people do when they disappear for years."

"I wanted to," he said. "But everything got messy. My aunt got sick, my dad stopped talking to me... I didn't have the words."

Her voice sharpened. "So you just *left*. No explanation. No goodbye."

"I didn't mean to hurt you, Em," he said softly. "I just... didn't know how to stay when everything around me was falling apart."

Her throat burned. "Well, you managed to find your way back. Looks like everything worked out for you."

"Not everything," he murmured.

She met his gaze, and the quiet between them pulsed with everything unsaid.

"Don't," she said under her breath.

"Don't what?"

"Look at me like that."

He grinned — slow, familiar, infuriating. "Can't help it. You still look like trouble."

Despite herself, Emma laughed, shaking her head. "Still blaming me for your burned caramel?"

"Always."

For a second, it was easy — too easy — and that scared her more than anything.

She gathered her tray, squaring her shoulders. "Well, good luck at the contest, Carter. You'll need it."

"Luck's for amateurs," he said with a wink. "But if you ever want to taste the competition, I'll save you a slice."

She huffed a laugh. "Keep dreaming."

As she turned to leave, Noah's voice followed softly after her — not teasing this time, but sincere. "It's good to see you again, Em."

And that, somehow, was worse than any flirtation.

Chapter 3

Caught in the Past

The next morning, Maplewood felt softer — like the whole town was stretching awake after a long nap. The smell of cinnamon and roasted pecans drifted through Main Street as shop windows glowed with golden light.

Emma Lawson stood outside her bakery, *Sugar & Spice*, a paper cup of coffee warming her hands. The glass panes were fogged from the heat inside, where trays of scones and pies cooled in neat rows. Business had been good lately — better than she'd dared to hope — but her mind wasn't on her success.

It was at a diner across the street.
 On *him.*

Through the glass, she could see Noah Carter moving behind the counter, sleeves rolled up, laughing with a customer. The same easy confidence. The same way he used to lean in too close when they baked together during the town fair years ago.

Hazel had stopped by earlier that morning, catching her staring through the window. "Oh no," she'd said with a knowing smirk. "We're not doing this, Em."

Emma tore her eyes away from the diner. "Doing what?"

"Mooning over him like he's the last slice of pie in the display case."

Emma rolled her eyes, though her heart betrayed her by thudding a little faster. "Please. I was just wondering if his coffee is as burnt as it used to be."

"Sure you were." Hazel's grin turned sly. "You know, the last time you baked with him, you almost kissed. The tension in that kitchen could've melted butter."

Emma's cheeks flushed. "That was years ago. I was twenty, he was twenty-one, and it was nothing."

Hazel tilted her head. "Mm-hmm. Are you sure about that? Because he's been glancing at this bakery window for the last five minutes."

Emma froze. Slowly — too slowly — she turned her head, and sure enough, Noah was leaning against the diner doorway, coffee mug in hand, looking straight at her with a crooked grin. He raised the cup in greeting.

"Don't wave back," Hazel hissed.

"I wasn't going to!"

But Emma *did* wave back — too quickly, too awkwardly — and Hazel groaned. "Girl, you are a lost cause."

"I'm fine," Emma said, her voice rising an octave as she ducked inside the bakery. "Completely fine."

Inside, the bell above the door jingled softly. Warm light flickered across rows of pastries and jars of pumpkin spice sugar. Emma tried to focus on her prep for the upcoming **Maplewood Harvest Bake-Off** — the event that would determine who claimed the title of the town's best baker.

For years, that title had belonged to her grandmother. Now, Emma was determined to win it in her honor.

But she hadn't counted on competing against the man who used to sneak into her kitchen for leftover pie crusts and kiss her cheek when she wasn't looking.

She leaned against the counter, staring down at the recipe cards. *Focus, Emma. He's just Noah. The one who left. The one who didn't come back until now.*

Still, when the bell over her door jingled again, her pulse betrayed her.

Noah Carter stepped inside, the scent of fresh coffee clinging to him, his smile slow and sure. "Morning, Lawson."

Her breath caught. "Morning."

"Thought I'd stop by. Heard the best baker in town was hiding her recipes from the competition."

"Maybe I just don't trust anyone who burns bacon for a living," she said, arching a brow.

He chuckled. "Still got that sharp tongue, huh?"

"And you still think charm fixes everything."

He leaned against the counter, his voice softening. "Doesn't fix everything. It just helps me survive the people I miss."

Emma's chest tightened. "Don't," she whispered.

"Don't what?"

"Say things like that."

He smiled, eyes warm but unreadable. "Then stop looking at me like you remember."

Her stomach fluttered, and she hated that it did. "You should go, Carter."

"I should," he said — but didn't move. "See you at the bake-off, Lawson."

When he left, the bell over the door chimed again, and Emma exhaled shakily, pressing a hand to her chest.

Hazel appeared from the back room, eyebrows raised. "So... that happened."

Emma groaned. "Don't start."

"Oh, I'm not starting," Hazel said with a grin. "I'm *documenting*. Because whatever that was? It's only getting worse."

Chapter 4

A Recipe for Tension

The Maplewood Farmer's Market buzzed with Saturday life — baskets of apples, fresh honey jars, the air rich with roasted pecans and laughter. Autumn leaves fluttered between booths like lazy confetti.

Emma Lawson moved through the crowd with purpose, her tote bag already half full. She scanned the produce stands, searching for the perfect pumpkin. It had to be firm, deep orange, and heavy enough to make her grandmother proud.

Hazel trailed beside her, sipping cider. "You've been inspecting these pumpkins like you're choosing a husband."

Emma smirked. "Pumpkin's more reliable."

Hazel snorted, "You say that now, but if *he* shows up, you'll be sniffing cinnamon and losing all sense of logic."

Emma ignored her — or tried to — as she knelt to check another pumpkin. Her fingers brushed the smooth surface just as another hand reached for the same one.

"Guess great minds think alike," a deep voice teased.

Her pulse jumped before she even looked up. Noah Carter stood over her, sleeves rolled up, the faintest grin curving his lips.

She straightened slowly, clutching the pumpkin like a shield. "Seriously? Do you just appear wherever I am now?"

He held up his own empty basket. "What can I say? The market's small. And apparently, so is the pumpkin selection."

Hazel stepped forward, grinning like she'd manifested this moment herself. "Oh, I'll just—go grab us more cider." She winked at Emma and disappeared into the crowd.

Emma narrowed her eyes. "You planned this."

"Hazel?" He chuckled. "Maybe. Me? No. But I'm not complaining."

Emma turned the pumpkin in her hands. "You always were good at showing up uninvited."

"Yeah, but back then, you didn't look like *this* when you saw me." His gaze drifted, not disrespectful—just noticing. The curve of her cheek, the smudge of flour still faint on her sleeve.

Emma's throat tightened. "Don't."

"Don't what?" he asked softly.

"Say things like that."

He took a small step closer, lowering his voice so only she could hear. "Then maybe stop looking at me like you want me to keep talking."

Her pulse fluttered. "You really think you're charming, don't you?"

"I don't think," he said, leaning just close enough for her to feel the warmth of his breath, "I *know*."

Emma huffed a laugh, brushing past him toward the next stall. "You haven't changed at all."

"Sure I have," he said, following with a slower pace. "I make a better pie crust now. Want me to prove it?"

She spun around, one eyebrow raised. "You trying to challenge me, Carter?"

"More like tempt you."

"Tempting me won't win you the bake-off."

He grinned, eyes gleaming. "Who says I'm trying to win the bake-off?"

For a moment, she froze, unsure if he meant the contest — or her.

Hazel returned just in time to interrupt whatever was about to happen. "Okay, what did I miss? You both look like someone turned the oven on too high."

Emma grabbed the cider. "We were just discussing competition."

"Uh-huh," Hazel said, clearly unconvinced. "Well, maybe keep the competition PG-rated in public."

Noah laughed, tipping his head toward Emma. "See you at the next round, Lawson. Don't let me distract you too much."

As he walked away, Hazel elbowed her. "You're in trouble."

"I am not," Emma said firmly, though her face betrayed her.

"Girl, you were about one cinnamon stick away from combusting."

Emma groaned, burying her face in her hands. "He's infuriating."

"Uh-huh," Hazel said, smirking. "And hot. Don't forget hot."

Chapter 5

Flour Fights & Lingering Looks

The Maplewood Community Center smelled like cinnamon, coffee, and a touch of nervous energy. Rows of folding tables lined the main hall, each one occupied by the town's best bakers — or, in Noah's case, a few brave souls with overconfidence and charm.

Emma Lawson stood at her booth, organizing her ingredients with clinical precision. Her grandmother's recipe cards were stacked neatly beside her mixing bowls. Every scoop of sugar, every swirl of pumpkin puree felt like a piece of legacy.

Hazel leaned on the edge of the table, chewing a piece of gum and watching the crowd. "You know, for someone who says she doesn't care about him, you've reorganized your display three times since he walked in."

"I'm making sure it's perfect," Emma said, flattening a dish towel that didn't need flattening.

"Uh-huh," Hazel said, popping her gum. "And the fact that you can see his table from this angle has nothing to do with it."

Emma didn't dignify that with a response. Instead, she focused on her pie crust, rolling it with care. She told herself it was just another contest. Just another bake.

But then *he laughed.*
A low, familiar sound that wrapped around her chest like a slow melody.

Noah Carter stood across the room, sleeves rolled up, apron tied loosely around his waist. He looked maddeningly relaxed, chatting with a group of elderly women who were clearly smitten. His booth — *Carter's Diner: Comfort Classics* — featured rustic pecan pies and warm apple tarts.

When his eyes finally found hers, his grin widened.

"Don't look at him," Hazel murmured, pretending to adjust the mixer.

"I'm not—" Emma's voice faltered as he winked. "—looking at him."

"Oh, you're *looking,* all right." Hazel nudged her gently. "And I think he knows it."

Tanisha Pollard

The contest organizer, Mrs. Pembroke, tapped the microphone at the front of the room. "Welcome, bakers! This year's Maplewood Harvest Bake-Off is officially underway. You have three hours to prepare your signature pie for judging. May your ovens stay hot and your crusts stay flaky!"

The crowd clapped, the hum of mixers and laughter filling the air.

Emma slipped into her rhythm — flour, butter, water — the sound of rolling pins and chatter blending into something almost meditative. Until...

"Need a hand with that crust?"

Noah's voice slid through her focus like silk.

She didn't look up. "Pretty sure it's illegal for contestants to interfere with their rivals."

"I was being neighborly."

"Don't you have your own pie to ruin?"

He laughed softly, leaning one elbow on the edge of her table. "You wound me, Lawson. I've improved since our last bake-off."

She glanced up at him, one brow raised. "Our *last* bake-off? You mean the county fair ten years ago when your crust collapsed, and you blamed the humidity?"

He grinned. "It *was* humid."

Emma tried not to smile, but failed. "You're impossible."

"And yet, here I am."

She huffed and turned back to her dough, sprinkling more flour on the counter. He didn't move.

"Seriously," she said, her tone sharp but her lips twitching, "you're in my space."

"Your space smells good," he replied. "And it's warmer over here."

She gave him a pointed look. "That's the oven, Carter."

"I know. Still applies."

Hazel, passing by with a tray of measuring cups, muttered under her breath, "Lord, give me strength. Or at least a spray bottle to cool these two down."

Emma shot her friend a glare, but Hazel only smirked and walked off.

Then, as if fate were conspiring against her, Noah reached for the same rolling pin she did. Their hands collided — palm to palm — a jolt of static snapping between them.

"Sorry," he murmured, though his eyes said otherwise.

"Don't," she warned softly. "Don't start."

"Start what?"

"That grin. That—"

Before she could finish, Hazel's elbow accidentally nudged a bag of flour off the edge of the table. It burst open like a white cloud, coating everything — and everyone — in reach.

Noah froze, blinking through the powdery haze. Then he laughed — *that* laugh again — deep and contagious.

Emma sputtered. "You did that on purpose!"

"Me? You think I'd sabotage your perfect pie setup?"

"You're standing in my flour cloud, Carter."

He grinned, his teeth bright against the dusting of white across his dark skin. "Guess we're even now."

She grabbed a pinch of flour from the table and flicked it toward him. "Now we're even."

The flour fight escalated fast — laughter, shrieks, a few scandalized gasps from nearby bakers. Noah held up his hands in surrender, still chuckling. "You're going to get us disqualified!"

"Good," she said, eyes sparkling. "Then I won't have to lose to you."

Their laughter faded into a breathless quiet. For one suspended heartbeat, they stood there — close enough to feel the warmth radiating between them. The noise of the contest dulled around them, the world narrowing to a single, charged space.

Hazel's voice broke the spell. "All right, lovebirds, some of us are trying to *bake* here!"

Emma jumped back, her cheeks flushed scarlet. Noah just smirked, brushing flour off his sleeve.

"See you at judging, Lawson," he said, his voice low enough that only she could hear. "Try not to miss me too much."

Emma exhaled hard. "You're insufferable."

Tanisha Pollard

He leaned in close, his grin wicked and soft all at once. "And yet, you still keep looking."

Chapter 6

Stirring the Past

The bakery smelled like a living postcard of autumn: warm cinnamon, roasted pecans, and butter mingled with the faint sharpness of nutmeg. Sunlight fell through the windows in soft beams, catching the dust motes dancing like tiny golden sparks. Emma moved through the kitchen with the precision of someone who had done this a thousand times, yet her heart thudded with a rhythm that had nothing to do with kneading dough.

Hazel burst in like a whirlwind, scarf tails fluttering and boots thudding against the wood floor. "Well, well! If it isn't the bakery goddess herself, pretending she's not thinking about *him*!"

It had been years since she'd seen Noah Carter, and yet every morning since his return, she'd caught herself half-expecting his reflection in the bakery window.

Emma's rolling pin paused mid-roll. "Hazel—"

"Oh, come on," Hazel interrupted, leaning over the counter and peering at her with mock seriousness. "You froze at the farmer's market. Legs like spaghetti. Eyes like you'd seen a ghost. That wasn't 'friendly,' Emma. That was caught off guard and swooning. Admit it."

Emma's face warmed. "I did not swoon. I... I'm focused on the pies. That's all."

Hazel smirked. "Sure, keep telling yourself that. Focused on pies. Right." She plucked a cinnamon stick off the counter, twirling it between her fingers. "You know, the way you keep looking at the front door like it's him... adorable."

Emma rolled her eyes, muttering, "I am not looking at the door."

Hazel's grin widened. "Denial looks *so good* on you. Too bad it's giving you away."

Emma's laugh came out too tight. Hazel had a way of peeling her open, layer by layer, until even her excuses sounded hollow.

The bell jingled as Mr. Hollingsworth, the elderly man from two blocks down, shuffled in, leaning heavily on his cane. "Good morning, Emma! One of those pumpkin scones, please."

"Coming right up," Emma said, forcing her hands to be steady. Her pulse jumped, though there was no reason it should have. She imagined Noah standing there instead, watching her hands move, the light catching in her hair.

Mr. Hollingsworth paid, oblivious to her racing heartbeat, and shuffled out. As the door shut, the silence was too loud — thick with the kind of loneliness that smelled like sugar and nostalgia. The shop felt suddenly empty; the walls echoing a warmth that wasn't just from the ovens. Emma wiped her hands on her apron and tried to focus, but every sound—the soft creak of the door, the faint hum of the mixer—made her expect him.

Hazel returned briefly, carrying a small basket of apples. "I swear, you blush faster than a kettle coming to a boil. I love it."

Emma groaned. "Hazel!"

"Shh. You know you like the attention. Admit it, Emma. You always liked the chase."

Emma turned away, kneading the dough harder. "It's just… memories. Nothing else."

She breathed in, letting the aroma of sugar and baked apples fill her lungs. Her fingers brushed against the cool wood of the counter, and a memory slipped unbidden—Noah leaning over the same counter years ago, laughing at something she'd said. Her pulse stuttered. She tried to focus on rolling the dough, but her body hummed with an awareness she refused to name.

Every creak of the door, every tiny noise, made her imagine him entering. The thought made her stomach flutter, heat creeping into her cheeks.

The scent of cinnamon blurred the edges of reality. For a heartbeat, the present dissolved, and her memory took over. The counter gleamed under her hands. Suddenly, the bakery faded from reality, replaced by the vision of him walking through the door, casual but commanding. His gaze found hers, steady, deliberate.

"You've changed," he murmured.

Emma's breath caught. His hand brushing a loose curl from her face, the warmth of his touch sent shivers down her spine. She pressed her hands into the cool wood of the counter she used every morning, grounding herself against the wave of heat rising inside her.

Pumpkin Pie & Piercing Hearts

And in the haze of flour and memory, the distance between fantasy and flesh disappeared. He leaned closer, lips brushing hers softly. The tension coiled, electric, thrilling. Her body betrayed her calm insistence, but her mind argued fiercely that this was impossible. She pulled away, wanting to deny him, but it was impossible. Pulling her back to him, he kissed her deeply, then lifted and placed her on the counter, kissing her repeatedly, causing her to softly moan. He took that as a sign to go on and began kissing her neck, sucking softly. He kissed her behind her ear, on that sweet spot that drove her crazy. She pulled him back to her lips, begging him not to stop. The rest blurred into heat, breath, and a heartbeat that wasn't entirely her own.

Bang! She snapped back with a gasp, realizing she'd knocked over a tray in her haste. Flour dusted the floor. "Not real," she muttered, patting the counter to collect herself. But her body didn't know the difference. Her lips still tingled, her pulse still raced, and part of her almost wished she hadn't woken up.

Hazel left the bakery to run some deliveries, which left the bakery silent. Emma was alone again, surrounded by the hum of the ovens and the ghosts of her own making. The warmth of the ovens and the scent of baking filled every corner. Emma stacked trays, dusted sugar off counters, and tried to force her mind to focus.

Every customer who entered felt like him, and every noise of the doorbell made her pulse quicken. She imagined his shoulders brushing hers as they reached for the same pumpkin, the laughter they would have shared, the lingering look before he disappeared again.

She tried to steady herself with a deep inhale, grounding in the cinnamon and warm butter. But nothing could mask the thrill coursing through her.

By the time Emma locked the doors and stepped into the crisp evening air, the tension in her chest hadn't eased. Streetlights cast long shadows across the quiet streets, and leaves rustled softly along the sidewalk, as though whispering secrets she wasn't ready to hear. Her mind kept circling back to that same touch she'd imagined — so vivid it left her aching, so wrong it left her restless.

At home, she moved through her nightly routine on autopilot—lighting a candle, hanging her apron, brushing flour from her hair. Everything felt unusually intimate tonight—the soft glow of the lamp, the faint hum of the fridge, the candle's slow flicker like a heartbeat.

The silence wasn't peace. It was absence. It was him. It was thick, heavy, waiting — the kind of quiet that made her remember every laugh she'd tried to forget.Sliding into bed, she pressed her cheek to the pillow and let out a slow breath. Her mind drifted to him again—the imagined brush of his shoulder, the press of his lips in the bakery daydream.

She'd spent months pretending she didn't miss him, pretending her body didn't still wake up remembering his weight beside her. But memory was cruel—it never needed permission to return.

The bed felt too big, too cold, and she hated how easily she could still feel his warmth there.

Somewhere between waking and sleep, a warmth pressed against her back—real enough to make her inhale sharply.

"Missed me?"

His voice slipped through the dark, smooth and sinful as a confession.

Emma's breath hitched. Her fingers clutched the edge of the blanket, heart hammering. "No... I mean... maybe," she whispered, voice trembling between disbelief and longing.

"I thought you might say that," the voice murmured, low, teasing, unmistakably his. "Funny... I've thought about you every day I've been gone."

Her pulse quickened. She could almost feel him there, his presence brushing against her side. "Noah..." she breathed, half in awe, half in defiance.

"Shhh," he replied softly, voice certain, intimate. "Just let me stay close for a minute. You know you want it."

Emma's hands clenched the sheets, mind screaming to resist, to stay in denial—but every nerve in her body betrayed her.

His weight dipped the bed, heat radiating from him like a secret she wasn't ready to face. "Just let me stay," he murmured, his breath teasing her ear. "You know you want me close."

She turned, trembling, her voice soft. "You left."

"I know," he whispered, brushing his thumb across her bottom lip. "And I've hated myself every night for it."

Pumpkin Pie & Piercing Hearts

The moment stretched between them, thick and waiting. When his lips met hers, the world cracked open. He kissed her like he was making up for lost time—slow, then hungry, tasting the words she never said out loud.

Her hands slid up his chest, relearning the lines of him. The scent of flour and vanilla still clung to her skin, mixing with the warmth of him until she could no longer tell where she ended and he began.

He tugged the strap of her nightgown down her shoulder, pressing his mouth to the bare skin he found there. His teeth grazed her collarbone, and she gasped, arching into him.

"Tell me this isn't just a dream," he whispered.

"If it is," she breathed, "don't wake me up."

Noah groaned—a low, broken sound—and claimed her mouth again, rougher this time. His hands moved down her body, mapping her curves with reverence and need. When his palm brushed between her thighs, she shuddered.

"Still so damn soft," he murmured, his voice dark and full of ache. "Still mine."

"Noah—" Her protest died when his fingers slipped beneath the lace of her thong, finding her slick and wanting. Her hips lifted toward him instinctively, a wordless plea.

"Look at me," he ordered softly.

She met his gaze—and nearly came undone from that alone. The way he looked at her wasn't just lust; it was history, apology, and devotion all tangled into one impossible thing.

He kissed down her stomach, slow and deliberate, leaving a trail of heat until his mouth hovered between her legs. His breath brushed her skin before his tongue did, teasing her until her hands clutched the sheets.

The first stroke of his tongue tore a sound from her she didn't recognize—raw and desperate. He groaned against her, his tongue flicking and circling until her thighs trembled around him.

"That's it," he whispered, voice muffled by her. "Let go for me."

When he sucked her clit, her vision went white. Her body arched off the bed, a cry escaping her throat as pleasure pulsed through her like lightning. He didn't stop. He kept her there, tasting every wave, every tremor, until she was shaking and begging his name.

Finally, he rose over her, his mouth glistening, his eyes dark and wrecked. "I've dreamed about you like this every night."

She reached for him, pulled him down to her. "Then stop dreaming," she whispered.

He entered her slowly, both of them gasping at the contact—at the way it felt like coming home and falling apart all at once.

Their movements found a rhythm, each thrust deeper, slower, desperate and tender all at once. Her nails dug into his back; his hand tangled in her hair. When he whispered her name like a prayer, she shattered again, crying out against his mouth as he followed her over the edge.

For a long time, neither spoke. Just breathing, tangled together, lost in the cruel magic of what couldn't be real.

When she blinked again, he was gone. The candle had burned low, wax pooling in the glass.
 He wasn't hers anymore. But he still haunted every corner of her body.

Outside, Maplewood slept under a quilt of fog, unaware that somewhere above the bakery, a woman dreamed of the man who once left—and never really did.

Chapter 7

Sweet as Cinnamon, Sharp as Clove

The morning rush at Carter's Diner buzzed like a well-rehearsed song—coffee cups clinking, bacon sizzling, the faint hum of the old jukebox in the corner.

 Noah Carter wiped his hands on a towel and leaned against the counter, watching the sunrise filter through the front windows. Maplewood was awake again, the streets lined with golden leaves and familiar faces he hadn't seen in a decade.

The same faces who had once watched him leave.

He'd been gone ten years, but walking through that diner door again had felt both foreign and inevitable. His aunt, Lila Carter, had left the place to him in her will. It wasn't just a business—it was her pride, her legacy. The floors still creaked in the same places she used to dance to Elvis while frying bacon. Her handwriting still labeled the pie tins in looping cursive: *Apple crumble, not too sweet.*

He could almost hear her voice teasing him.
"You've got my hands, kid. Just use 'em for something worth staying for."

He hadn't understood that back then. At twenty-one, he'd thought leaving Maplewood was the only way to matter.
Now he wasn't sure what mattered more than this—than the smell of coffee, the sound of laughter, and the woman across the street whose bakery light was already glowing at dawn.

Through the diner window, he could see her. Emma Lawson, head down, hair pulled into a messy bun, moving with the same fierce focus she always had. He remembered her like this—hands dusted with flour, humming softly under her breath, completely in her element.

Noah smiled faintly. *Same Emma. Just sharper now. Stronger.*

"Boss?" Joe, his line cook, broke the moment. "You good? You've been staring out that window for a solid minute. We burnin' the bacon or you burnin' for someone?"

Noah shot him a look. "Mind your eggs, Joe."

Joe grinned. "Uh-huh. Just sayin'—girl's been killin' it over there. Half the town's talking about those pies. You're gonna let her outshine you, boss?"

"She already does," Noah murmured.

"Damn. Didn't realize it was that deep."

Noah chuckled, shaking his head. "It's not. She's just... something else."

He busied himself refilling a pot of coffee, but his thoughts wouldn't stop circling. He hadn't planned on running into Emma so soon. He hadn't planned on *feeling* this much, this fast. The moment he saw her at the farmer's market—eyes wide, voice sharp, still radiating that same fire—it had knocked him flat.

And now, every morning, he found himself looking toward the bakery like a habit he couldn't break.

Joe leaned his elbows on the counter. "So, what actually happened, huh? You left town, made it big somewhere, then what—came back for nostalgia?"

Noah hesitated. "Something like that."

But the truth was heavier. He hadn't "made it big." He'd burned out. The restaurant he opened in the city had crashed within two years—too much pressure, too much noise, too many people who wanted his recipes but not his heart. He'd come home with nothing but a few scars and a letter from his aunt he found tucked in her recipe box:

If you're reading this, you finally stopped running. This place will take care of you if you take care of it. And maybe—if you're lucky—it'll give you a reason to stay.

He'd laughed when he read it. Now it felt less like a joke and more like a prophecy.

The bell over the door chimed. Hazel breezed in, scarf trailing, a mischievous grin already forming. "Are you planning to keep staring out that window or actually eat breakfast today?"

"Hazel," he said, chuckling. "You're supposed to be helping Emma, not harassing me."

"I can multitask," she said, sliding onto a stool. "Besides, she's pretending not to care about you, which means she cares way too much. Thought I'd do a little recon."

"Recon?"

She leaned forward conspiratorially. "She's been baking like a woman possessed. Won't stop talking about the contest. Or you. Especially you."

Noah arched an eyebrow. "Really?"

Hazel grinned. "Oh yeah. She hates that you're back. Hates how you make her laugh. Hates how good you look behind a counter. Totally hates you."

He laughed softly. "You're not helping."

"Wasn't trying to. I like chaos." Hazel winked, snagging a piece of toast from the counter. "Just don't screw it up this time, Carter."

She left as quickly as she came, leaving the faint scent of cinnamon and gossip in her wake.

Noah turned back to the window, the smile slowly fading from his lips. *Don't screw it up this time.*

He watched as Emma rearranged the pie display in her front window. She didn't look up, didn't notice him—but he noticed her. The way her brow furrowed when she concentrated. The way her hand brushed the counter like she was steadying herself.

He wanted to believe he'd come back just for the diner. But that was only half the truth. The other half stood right across the street, dusted in flour and impossible to forget.

Chapter 8

The Pie that Binds

The soft chime above the bakery door broke through the hum of the mixer. Emma looked up from her station, brushing a stray curl from her forehead. Noon sunlight streamed in through the big front window, catching the faint dusting of flour on her cheek.

Her heart stuttered. Noah Carter stood in the doorway, leaning casually against the frame like he had every right to be there — like he hadn't been gone for a decade.

He wore a crisp white button-up rolled to the elbows, black slacks, and a clean apron looped over one shoulder — clearly just coming from the diner. He looked comfortable. Confident. *Too* confident.

Emma's pulse jumped, but her voice came out steady.
 "We're closed until one. If you're looking for coffee, you've got a whole diner for that."

His mouth twitched. "I'm not here for coffee."

She turned back to her dough, keeping her hands busy. "Then what are you here for?"

"Delivery," he said simply, setting down a brown paper bag. "Hazel said you haven't eaten all day. She bribed me with a slice of pecan pie to make sure you did."

Emma blinked, caught off guard. "You're delivering food for Hazel now?"

"Temporary arrangement," he said with a grin. "I owed her a favor. Apparently, she cashes them in whenever she wants."

"Seems she's got you wrapped around her finger."

"Hazel? Nah." He leaned against the counter, eyes glinting. "You, maybe."

Her rolling pin stilled. "You think that's charming?"

"I think it's honest."

Emma let out a low exhale, steady but sharp. "You don't get to walk in here with that smirk like nothing happened."

His smile faltered. "I never said nothing happened."

For a moment, neither of them spoke. The air between them thickened with something unspoken — regret, maybe. Or the ghost of ten years gone too fast.

Finally, she asked quietly, "Why'd you really come back, Noah?"

He hesitated, eyes flicking to the window, where sunlight glowed across the flour-dusted counter. "My aunt left me the diner. After she passed, it didn't feel right to sell it. Figured maybe I owed this town something. Maybe I owed *myself* a second chance."

Emma looked down, tracing the edge of the counter with her fingertip. "You could've had a second chance anywhere."

"Maybe. But not with you anywhere else."

Her breath caught. He said it softly, like a confession he hadn't planned to make.

"I didn't come back expecting things to be the same," he continued. "But walking into the market that day—seeing you? It felt like I'd never really left."

Emma swallowed, trying to stay firm. "You did leave, Noah. You left and didn't look back."

"I did," he said quietly. "Every damn day."

Silence stretched between them, fragile and heavy. The only sound was the rhythmic hum of the oven and the heartbeat pounding in her ears.

Emma turned back to her dough. "You should probably go before Hazel decides to send you back with another chore."

He didn't move. "You always did get mean when you're scared."

Her head snapped up. "I'm not scared."

"Could've fooled me."

Something sharp cracked between them — frustration, longing, history. She reached for the flour tin too quickly, her hand brushing his. Heat sparked up her arm like an electric current. He caught her wrist before she could pull away.

"Emma," he said softly, voice low and rough. "You don't have to keep pretending."

"I'm not pretending."

"Yeah, you are. I see it in the way you look at me — like you're mad I left, but angrier that I came back."

Her pulse thundered in her ears. "You think you know everything, don't you?"

"No," he murmured, stepping closer. "But I know you."

The air shifted. Her back brushed against the counter as he leaned in, close enough for her to smell the faint scent of coffee and cinnamon on his shirt.

"Tell me I'm wrong," he whispered.

Emma's throat tightened. Her voice came out barely a breath. "You're wrong."

"Liar."

She tried to turn away, but his hand was still around her wrist — not tight, just grounding. Her breath hitched. The dough on the counter was forgotten. The pie crust, the rolling pin, the clock — all of it faded.

What remained was that same pulse, that same spark that had been haunting her since the market.

For a heartbeat, she thought he might kiss her —
and for another, she wanted him to.

But instead, he let go. The warmth of his touch
lingered, burning where his hand had been.

He stepped back, his voice steady again. "Eat
something before you faint. Hazel will kill me if
you don't."

And just like that, he was gone. The bell above the
door chimed softly in his wake, leaving behind only
the scent of him and the thundering of her own
heart.

Emma stared at the empty space where he'd stood.
"Damn you, Noah Carter," she whispered.

Then, almost against her will, she reached for the
bag he'd brought. Inside was a perfectly wrapped
breakfast sandwich and a note in his handwriting:

You still forget to eat when you're mad. —
N.

Her chest ached and fluttered all at once.
The pie in front of her blurred, the crust smearing
under her palm.

She hated him for knowing her so well.

Chapter 9

Cracks in the Crust

The morning light filtered through the bakery window, painting warm gold across the countertops and the soft rise of flour-dusted dough. The scent of cinnamon, sugar, and roasted pecans wrapped around Emma Lawson like a memory she didn't mean to revisit. Her hands moved on instinct—press, fold, turn—but her thoughts were far from Maplewood's sleepy main street.

It had started again. The same flutter she thought she'd buried years ago. The same restless energy that came whenever Noah Carter was near.

She told herself it was the contest, the pressure, the late nights and early mornings. But she knew better.

The past had a way of sneaking in—through the smell of baked apples, through the way his laugh echoed when he teased her, through the glances that lingered too long over the rolling pin and sugar bowl.

Years earlier, the first spark had been just as unexpected.

It was at the Maplewood school fair. She had been standing behind the charity pie booth, her cheeks flushed pink from the oven's heat and her nerves. Her apron was too big, her curls had escaped her ponytail, and her hands shook as she rolled out a crust that refused to cooperate.

Then he'd appeared—Noah Carter, sleeves rolled up, grin lazy and confident, like he had all the time in the world to watch her struggle.

"I didn't know you could bake like this," he'd said, leaning over the table, elbows resting on the wood. His voice had been teasing, but there was something curious behind it.

Emma had tried to play it off. "It's just pies," she'd said, focusing on her rolling pin. But her pulse had given her away.

He chuckled, brushing a fleck of flour from the counter. "Just pies? Lawson, you've been standing here since morning like you're training for a pastry marathon."

She'd looked up then, ready to roll her eyes, but his gaze caught hers—steady, warm, amused. Her stomach had flipped so hard she nearly dropped the pie crust.

When his elbow brushed hers as he reached for a pie plate, it was such a small thing. Accidental. Forgettable. But the spark it sent through her fingers lingered long after he'd walked away.

That spark was what made her notice him everywhere after that—across the cafeteria, leaning against lockers, sitting two rows over in English class. They weren't friends, not really. But there were *moments.* Tiny, fragile things that she tucked away and pretended didn't matter.

She remembered the afternoons in the library, pretending to study, their heads bent over the same textbook. When he passed her a pen, his fingers brushed hers. When he whispered a joke, she couldn't stop smiling. And once—just once—he rested his hand on hers when reaching for a notebook. It had been half a second, but she'd felt it for weeks.

There had been that night behind the gym, too. The autumn festival. Music and laughter floating from inside. She had been helping clean up, her hands still sticky with caramel. He'd shown up, hands in his pockets, that same half-smile playing at his lips.

"You missed the dance," he'd said.

"I had pies to finish," she replied.

"Of course you did," he teased, stepping closer. "You always pick work over fun."

She'd rolled her eyes, but her heart was thudding hard enough to drown out the music. "And you always pick trouble."

He'd grinned, leaning closer until she could smell soap and cinnamon gum. "Maybe I like trouble."

Their eyes had met. The air had gone still. He could have kissed her then—should have, maybe—but he hadn't.

And that was the thing about Noah Carter. He always stopped just short of what she wanted him to do.

Emma blinked, the smell of cinnamon dragging her back to the present. The oven timer beeped, slicing through the memory. She exhaled, pressing her palms into the dough to steady herself. The past wasn't supposed to matter. She was over it. She was building something new, something steady.

Except... Now he was back.

And every time he looked at her across the contest table, every time his fingers brushed hers reaching for the same bowl, she felt sixteen again—fluttery, flustered, and entirely out of control.

"Seems like we're always reaching for the same things," he'd said last night, his voice low and teasing.

She'd wanted to laugh it off, but her heart had betrayed her. "Some things never change," she'd murmured instead.

Now, standing in her bakery, sunlight glowing against her skin, Emma felt the echo of those words like a challenge.

Noah Carter had left Maplewood right after graduation—without a goodbye, without an explanation. She'd watched him drive away from her grandmother's porch, his taillights disappearing into the night, and told herself she would never think about him again.

But life had a cruel sense of humor. Years later, here he was—older, sharper around the edges, carrying the same smirk and a thousand unspoken apologies in his eyes.

Tanisha Pollard

Across town, Noah Carter leaned against the counter of his diner, staring into a cup of coffee that had long gone cold. The sound of the storm still echoed faintly in his memory—the night they'd shared laughter, flour fights, and something dangerously close to a kiss.

He'd thought time would dull it, that the girl he'd left behind would fade like a childhood dream. But every time he saw her now—hair tied back, sleeves rolled, fire in her voice—he felt that same pull.

He remembered the library afternoons, her quiet laugh, the way her lip caught between her teeth when she was nervous. He'd wanted to tell her back then—before the scholarship, before leaving—that she was the reason he came to the fair at all.

But he hadn't said a word.

Now he wished he had.

Watching her move around her bakery today, confident and untouchable, he realized the truth: she had built everything he'd been too scared to fight for.

And maybe—just maybe—he'd come back to try again.

Pumpkin Pie & Piercing Hearts

Emma reached for the cinnamon jar, and Noah's hand brushed hers as he stopped by the counter. Her pulse stuttered, that old electricity sparking again like no time had passed at all.

"Some things never change," she said quietly, her voice steadier than her heart.

"No," he said, eyes catching hers. "Some things just finally get a second chance."

Flour floated between them like tiny stars in the warm light. The air smelled of sugar and nostalgia. The ache, the pull, the what-ifs—they were all still there, simmering beneath the surface.

And for the first time, Emma didn't look away.

Chapter 10

Confessions over Caramel

The late afternoon sunlight slanted through the bakery windows, painting the flour-dusted counters in shades of amber and gold. The contest was only two days away, and Emma Lawson's kitchen buzzed with the rhythm of whisking, pouring, and tasting — and with the tension of trying not to look at the man currently leaning against her counter.

Noah Carter had shown up an hour ago "just to check on his rival," but he hadn't moved since. His sleeves were rolled up, revealing strong forearms dusted with flour, and his grin carried that same quiet mischief that had once made her forget her own name.

"Don't you have a diner to run?" she asked, measuring sugar with unnecessary precision.

He shrugged. "Joe's covering for me. Besides, your baking's more entertaining."

Emma glanced at him, unimpressed. "You mean more competitive."

"I mean dangerous," he countered smoothly. "You get this look when you're concentrating—like you're plotting to take over the world with a whisk."

She tried not to smile, but failed. "You're ridiculous."

"Maybe," he said, lowering his voice. "But you like ridiculous."

Her pulse fluttered. "In your dreams."

A pause. Then he smirked, soft and knowing. "Maybe."

✳✳✳

Hazel had left an hour ago, claiming she had "errands" but shooting Emma a look that said *don't do anything I wouldn't do.* The bakery felt quieter now — too quiet. The air was thick with the smell of sugar and simmering caramel, and every so often, Emma caught herself glancing at Noah, only to find him already watching her.

It shouldn't have been this easy to fall back into old rhythms. Their banter fits like a well-worn apron: familiar, comfortable, but dangerous when left too close to an open flame.

Emma poured the golden caramel into a pan, the liquid sugar gleaming under the light. "You're distracting me," she said without looking up.

"Good," Noah replied. "You're always so serious when you bake. It's like watching a general plan for war."

"This *is* war," she said, grabbing a spoon. "And I intend to win."

He stepped closer, so close she could feel the warmth radiating from him. "You're already winning," he murmured, his gaze dropping briefly to her lips.

Emma's hand trembled. She set the spoon down and stepped back. "Don't," she whispered, barely trusting her voice. "Not here."

"Why not here?" he asked softly. "Seems fitting. You and me. Flour. Sugar. Fire."

Her throat tightened. "Because I need to focus."

"On baking?" His grin deepened. "Or on pretending you don't still feel this?"

Her pulse stuttered, and the smell of burnt sugar snapped her back. "Damn it," she hissed, pulling the pan off the burner. "See what you made me do?"

Pumpkin Pie & Piercing Hearts

Noah chuckled, taking the spoon from her hand. "I think I made you feel something, actually."

She glared. "You're insufferable."

"Persistent," he corrected. He dipped a finger into the caramel — still warm, thick, golden — and blew on it before holding it out to her. "Taste."

She hesitated. "It's too hot."

"Trust me," he said, his tone suddenly quiet, earnest. "You'll like it."

Emma's breath caught as she leaned forward. She could smell the sugar and butter, could feel the heat of his skin just inches away. When her lips brushed his finger, a shiver ran through her entire body. The caramel was sweet and smooth — but not half as intoxicating as the look in his eyes.

Her voice came out softer than she intended. "Still think you can beat me?"

He grinned, a flash of boyish charm under the tension. "I think I'm already losing."

✱✱✱

They fell into silence then — not awkward, but heavy with meaning. The oven hummed softly in the background, and the clock on the wall ticked in slow, deliberate beats. It felt like time itself had slowed to watch them.

Emma stirred another batch of caramel just to have something to do with her hands. "You never said why you left," she said finally, her voice low.

He froze, mid-motion. For a moment, all the teasing drained from his face. "I didn't just leave for no reason, Emma. Back then… I thought I needed to prove something. I wanted more than this town could give me. I wanted to build something of my own."

Emma's eyes flicked to his, searching. "So you left to chase a dream."

He nodded once. "Yeah. I left to open a restaurant in the city. I thought if I made it big — if I could build something with my own hands — it would finally mean I was good enough." He let out a breath that sounded like defeat. "And for a while, it worked. Investors, reviews, packed tables… until it didn't."

Her heart twisted. "What happened?"

He smiled, but it didn't reach his eyes. "The burnout. The pressure. I stopped cooking because I loved it and started cooking because I was terrified to fail. And when everything fell apart — when the restaurant closed — I realized I'd built a life that had no real joy in it. Just noise."

Emma's fingers tightened around the handle of her mixing spoon. "So, you came back here."

He nodded slowly. "Yeah. My aunt passed away last winter. The diner was hers, and I couldn't let it close too. I came back to run it for her at first, but the truth is… I couldn't stay away from Maplewood anymore."

Her breath caught. "Because of her?"

"No," he said softly, eyes locking on hers. "Because of you."

The words landed between them, quiet but heavy. The caramel simmered low and slow on the stove, filling the room with warmth, sweetness, and something almost electric.

Emma swallowed hard. "You think you can just come back after all this time and—"

"I don't expect forgiveness," he interrupted gently. "I just needed you to know why. I didn't leave because I stopped caring, Emma. I left because I didn't think I was enough."

She looked at him for a long moment, her heartbeat loud in her ears. "And now?"

He smiled faintly, a little sad, a little hopeful. "Now I'm trying to be the kind of man who doesn't run away."

***

Hazel's voice came faintly from the front of the bakery: "Emma, you decent back there? I brought coffee!"

Emma startled, stepping back so quickly she nearly dropped the pan. "Perfect timing," she muttered.

Noah laughed quietly, the spell broken. "Guess that's my cue."

As he turned to leave, she caught his sleeve. "Noah."

He looked back, brows lifted.

"Thank you," she said softly. "For telling me."

He nodded once. "For the record, I never stopped thinking about you. Even when I tried."

And before she could find words, he was gone — out the door, the bell chiming behind him, leaving the scent of caramel and something else she couldn't quite name.

Emma stood in the quiet bakery, heart hammering, hand still warm from where he'd touched her. For the first time since he'd come back to Maplewood, she wasn't angry anymore.

Just afraid — because falling for him again felt a lot like burning caramel: slow, sticky, and impossible to control once it started.

Chapter 11

The First Taste

The morning after the caramel confession dawned soft and golden, sunlight stretching lazily across Maplewood. The bakery windows fogged gently as the first pies of the day baked, filling the air with pumpkin, brown sugar, and butter. Emma Lawson moved with her usual rhythm—measuring, whisking, rolling—but her thoughts weren't on the dough.

They were still tangled up in Noah Carter.

Every word from last night echoed like a heartbeat. *Because of you.*
She'd barely slept. She'd replayed that moment a dozen times—his voice, low and rough, his gaze steady when he said her name. It shouldn't have

affected her like this. He'd hurt her once before, and she'd promised herself she wouldn't fall again.

And yet… here she was, checking the clock every few minutes, half expecting him to walk through the door.

The bell above the entrance jingled. Her breath hitched. But it wasn't Noah.

"Emma Jean Lawson, do you ever take a break?" her mother's voice rang out, smooth as honey but sharp around the edges.

Emma turned, relief and fond exasperation flooding her all at once. "Morning, Mama."

Cynthia Lawson—impeccably dressed, brown-skinned elegance wrapped in a camel trench coat and pearls—strode into the bakery like she owned it. Her eyes swept over the counters, the displays, and finally her daughter, as if checking for dust. "This place smells like heaven. You've outdone yourself again."

"Thank you," Emma said, brushing her hands on her apron. "Coffee?"

Her mom smiled knowingly. "Always."

Emma poured her a cup, watching her mother's rings glint in the morning light. Cynthia took a sip, sighed contentedly, then turned a sharp eye on her daughter. "You look tired."

"Thanks," Emma said dryly. "That's exactly what I was going for."

"You've been working too much," Cynthia said, setting her cup down. "Your grandmother would tell you the same thing. God rest her soul, that woman loved this bakery, but she also loved her naps."

Emma smiled faintly. "Yeah, well. I inherited the baking, not the napping."

Her mom gave her a look. "You inherited her stubbornness too."

They shared a brief laugh, soft and familiar. Moments like this were rare—comfortable and easy. But as always, her mother didn't stay gentle for long.

"So," Cynthia began, stirring her coffee slowly, "tell me about this contest. And this… rival of yours."

Emma's stomach dipped. "What rival?"

Her mother's brow arched. "Hazel said you've been spending a lot of time with a certain Noah Carter.

The same Noah Carter who made my daughter blush through half of high school?"

Emma groaned. "Hazel needs to learn the meaning of privacy."

Cynthia's smile was far too amused. "So it is *Noah*."

"Yes," Emma said, too quickly. "He's back in town. He owns the diner now. We're both competing in the Thanksgiving Bake-Off."

Her mother hummed. "And?"

"And nothing," Emma said firmly, turning back to her dough.

Cynthia leaned against the counter, watching her with a smirk that was all too familiar. "You can tell me, baby. You used to talk about that boy like he hung the moon."

"That was a long time ago."

"Mm-hmm," her mother said, unconvinced. "And yet, you're turning red right now."

"I'm *hot,* Mama. The ovens are on."

Her mother chuckled softly, sipping her coffee. "You know, I always thought you two might end up together someday. You were so shy back then, always hiding behind your baking. He brought out your spark."

Emma's hands stilled. "He also left without saying goodbye."

Cynthia's expression softened. "I remember. You were heartbroken for weeks."

"Months," Emma muttered. "But that doesn't matter anymore."

Her mother's tone was gentle. "Are you sure about that?"

Emma turned away, staring at the sunlight streaming through the window. "He's different now. And so am I. I'm focused on the bakery and the contest. That's all that matters."

Cynthia smiled knowingly. "Sweetheart, you can be focused on success *and* open to love. Those two things aren't enemies."

"I'm not—" Emma began, then stopped. She could feel the denial forming, but the words refused to come out. Her throat tightened. "I'm not ready."

Her mother reached out, brushing a flour-smudge from Emma's cheek. "No one's ever really ready for love, baby. We just decide it's worth the risk."

For a moment, the kitchen was quiet except for the hum of the ovens. Emma swallowed hard, wishing she could believe that.

Then, mercifully, Hazel burst through the door, saving her from another round of motherly wisdom. "Morning, sunshine!" she chirped. "Oh! Hi, Mrs. Lawson! You look stunning as always."

Cynthia beamed. "Hazel, darling. You're the only one who notices."

Hazel grinned. "Please, I notice *everything.* Especially the look on Emma's face when Noah Carter walks into a room."

Emma shot her a glare sharp enough to cut glass. "Hazel."

Hazel held up her hands. "Just saying! That man has been in here more than the mailman this week."

Her mother arched an eyebrow. "Is that so?"

"I'm leaving," Emma declared, snatching her coat off the hook.

"Oh, no you don't," Hazel said, blocking the door. "We've got deliveries to make for the contest setup. You're stuck with me, sweetheart."

Cynthia laughed softly, shaking her head. "You two remind me of me and your grandmother. Always bickering, always baking."

As Hazel and Emma gathered their boxes, her mother touched her arm gently. "Just... don't let fear make you miss something good, Emma."

Emma nodded, her throat tight. "I'll try."

But as she stepped out into the cool air, the scent of pumpkin and spice following her, she wasn't thinking about pies or contests anymore.
 She was thinking about caramel.
 About a man who used to make her laugh.
 And about how dangerous it felt to want something that had already burned her once before.

Chapter 12

Secrets in the Kitchen

The bell over the door at Carter's Diner gave a weak jingle as the last customer left, and Noah leaned against the counter, rolling his shoulders. The scent of grilled onions and coffee clung to him—so different from the warmth of cinnamon and butter that seemed to follow Emma everywhere.

The diner had seen better days. One of the neon letters outside flickered stubbornly, the "R" in *Carter's* stuttering like a failing heartbeat. A fryer hissed in protest, and the radio in the corner warbled out an old love song that made Noah pause mid-wipe on the counter.

He sighed, pressing his thumb and forefinger to his eyes. Maplewood had changed little. But *he* had—and so had Emma Lawson.

He thought about the way she'd brushed flour off her cheek during practice last week, how her laughter had burst free like sunlight through a storm cloud. He had once thought that she smiled only for him. But now, watching her from a distance—seeing her command her bakery with confidence and passion—he realized she'd grown into something luminous. Something untouchable.

The door to the kitchen creaked, and his head cook, Benny, poked his head out. "Are you leaving soon, boss?" The fryer's giving us trouble again."

"Yeah, I'll look at it in the morning," Noah muttered. He glanced at the clock—10:47 p.m. Too late to be thinking about her. Too late to be thinking about the way she used to look at him, like he could change her entire world.

But curiosity was a dangerous thing.

Before he could talk himself out of it, Noah hung up his apron, grabbed his jacket, and stepped into the crisp night air.

Across town, light still poured from the windows of Emma's bakery.

Through the front glass, he could see her—hair tied up, apron dusted with sugar, brow furrowed in fierce concentration. She was testing a new caramel glaze, her movements fluid and sure, like the kitchen had become an extension of her.

Noah lingered across the street, hands in his pockets, unseen. There was something magnetic about watching her work. No audience, no pretense—just Emma and her craft. She was humming softly, a tune that drifted faintly through the glass. His pulse quickened as he noticed the way her brow furrowed when concentrating, the slight tilt of her head as she tasted the glaze. Every tiny movement was a message he ached to decipher.

For a moment, he let himself imagine walking inside, offering to help, standing beside her like they used to in the old community kitchen during high school fundraisers. The memory of her elbow brushing his arm, of laughter over spilled batter—it hit him with a quiet ache.

He saw her reach for a bowl, her fingers trembling slightly as she tasted the caramel. Then her lips curved into a small, satisfied smile. That smile nearly undid him.

He exhaled, the breath fogging in the cold air.

She doesn't need you, Carter, he told himself. *She's doing just fine without you.*

But deep down, he wasn't sure if he was trying to convince himself—or the ghost of the boy who left Maplewood thinking he could outrun what he felt for her.

A clatter broke the stillness. Inside, a pan slipped from Emma's hand, hitting the floor. She cursed softly, then laughed at herself. The sound—soft, real, unguarded—wrapped around him like a spell.

Before he knew it, he'd crossed the street.

The bell chimed softly when he stepped inside. Emma looked up, startled, her eyes widening for just a second before she schooled her expression into something neutral.

"Noah," she drawled. "The diner closed early?"

"Something like that," he replied, his voice rougher than intended. "Do you always work this late?"

She shrugged, turning back to her caramel. "Perfection doesn't keep office hours."

"Perfection, huh?" He stepped closer, watching the amber swirl coat her spoon. "You've always had a thing for caramel, haven't you?"

Her lips twitched. "You remember that?"

"I remember a lot of things," he breathed.

The words hung between them—unspoken years, regret, longing.

Emma cleared her throat, reaching for another pan. "If you're here for sweets, you'll have to wait till morning. The kitchen's closed."

"I wasn't here for sweets," he said before he could stop himself.

Her hand froze midair. She looked at him, searching his face for the truth behind the words. But Noah just smiled faintly and leaned against the counter.

Because the real sweetness was right before him, veiled in sugar and moonlight. Emma's pulse fluttered when he stepped closer; she could smell the faint traces of diner grease mixed with his cologne. Every step he took made her aware of her own heartbeat, and she had to remind herself to breathe.

Emma

The silence after he left felt heavier than the sound of his voice.

Emma stood in the middle of her bakery, spoon still in hand, the air around her thick with sugar and something else—something headier. She could almost feel his presence lingering in the room: the warmth where he'd stood, the faint trace of his cologne tangled with the scent of caramel.

Her heart thudded. She'd told herself she'd stopped caring. That the boy who left Maplewood didn't matter anymore. But seeing him there, watching her like she was the only thing still tethering him to this town—it made her breath catch in her throat.

She set the spoon down and forced herself to move. Wiping the counters. Locking up. Going through the motions of closing. But every time her eyes caught the reflection in the window, she half-expected to see him standing there again.

When she finally turned off the lights, the bakery felt too quiet. Too still.

She whispered into the dark, "You were the one who left, not me."
And even as the words left her lips, they trembled. Because a part of her—deep and buried—had never really let him go.

Pumpkin Pie & Piercing Hearts

By the time he got home, exhaustion had sunk deep into his bones. He dropped his keys onto the counter, kicked off his boots, and stood in the middle of his dimly lit kitchen for a long moment. The day clung to him—the grease, the noise, the ache in his shoulders. But underneath it all was *her*: the smell of caramel and vanilla ghosting along his skin.

He peeled off his shirt, leaving it on a chair, and headed for the bathroom. Steam filled the air as he turned on the shower, letting the water pound against his neck and back. It should have washed everything away—the stress, the longing—but it only made it worse.

The memory of her fingers brushing his arm, of her laughter curling around him, was like fire licking at his skin. He knew it was reckless to dwell on it, but the ache between desire and restraint was too sharp to ignore.

He tilted his head back beneath the spray, closing his eyes. The sound of water blurred into the memory of her laughter. For a split second, he saw her again in the bakery, light haloing her hair, lips parted as she teased him about perfection.

He shut off the water abruptly, bracing his hands on the tile, breathing hard. "Get a grip," he muttered.

Wrapped in a towel, he padded to his bedroom, the wooden floor cool beneath his feet. He collapsed onto the bed; the springs sighing under his weight. The room was dark except for the faint glow from the streetlight outside.

He was too tired to fight it anymore.

As his eyes drifted shut, the line between exhaustion and longing blurred.

At first, it was the bakery again—warm light, the smell of cinnamon, Emma's silhouette framed by the glow from the ovens. She turned toward him, soft and sure, her gaze meeting him with something that felt like an invitation.

And when she whispered his name, the sound pulled him under completely.

"Noah, do you know how much you haunted my dreams? Or how much I want to please you?" she whispered sultrily.

"Oh really, why don't you show me just how much?" he replied.

Emma swayed over to him. She kissed him, a deep kiss, as she looked into his eyes, as though daring herself. Her chest rose and fell rapidly; she felt his desire as a tangible weight pressing against her, and it made her pulse race with both fear and exhilaration.

She broke apart the kiss and dropped to her knees. She looked up at him, smirking. Then she unzipped his pants and pulled his boxers along with the pants down. His erect cock sprang up, anticipating its need.

"Emma, are you sure?" he had barely gotten the question out before Emma ran her tongue over the length of him.

"Fuckkk Emma."

Emma smiled up at him. Then she took him all the way to the hilt. Breathing deeply through her nose, she bobbed her head up and down, taking all of him repeatedly.

Noah groaned. He was fighting the urge to take over. "Christ, Emma, your mouth feels so fucking good."

Emma hollowed her cheeks and sucked him hard.

Noah lost it and grabbed the back of her head and pushed himself all the way down her throat. Her gag reflex kicking in caused him to groan. He pulled out so she could catch her breath. He then fucked her mouth mercilessly. Emma placed her hands on his thighs and let him use her mouth to please him.

Noah knew it was a matter of time before he would cum. His mind swirled with the memory of her smile, the curve of her waist, the warmth of her breath on his skin. Desire and need had entwined completely—there was no turning back. He fucked her mouth even faster, his movements now jerky as he began to cum down her throat.

"Emma, I want you to swallow every single drop," he whispered.

She listened like the good girl she was and swallowed every single drop. He pulled his spent cock out of her mouth and pulled her up.

"Such a fucking good girl," he said before he looked at her pink swollen lips and kissed her deeply.

Noah woke with a sharp inhale, the sound catching in his throat. His legs were tangled in the sheets, and sweat slicked his body. For a moment, disorientation kept him pinned — his mind still half in the dream, still caught in the scent of vanilla and caramel, in the feel of her hands on his skin.

Then the sunlight cut across the room, pale and cold, and reality hit like a bucket of ice water.

He dragged a hand over his face and groaned. "Jesus Christ, Carter…"

It wasn't the first time Emma Lawson had haunted his sleep, but it was the first time it had felt *that real*. Every detail clung to him — the warmth of her breath, the whisper of her voice, the way she'd looked at him with a hunger that matched his own. He sat up slowly, pressing his palms into his eyes as if he could scrub the image away.

The clock on his nightstand read 7:16 a.m. The diner would need him in an hour, but all he could think about was the ghost of her laughter echoing in his head.

"Great," he muttered, throwing his legs over the side of the bed. "Dream about the one woman you can't have and expect to make pancakes for tourists like nothing happened."

He pushed himself up and trudged toward the kitchen, rubbing the back of his neck. Coffee. He needed coffee and maybe something stronger.

As the machine hissed to life, he leaned against the counter, staring at the small window over the sink. From here, he could see the faint outline of downtown Maplewood — the church steeple, the rows of redbrick shops, and, just beyond that, the sign for *Sugar & Spice Bakery.*

Even from this distance, it taunted him.

He sipped the coffee, bitter and black, and tried to shake the image of her from his mind. But it was useless. The dream had burrowed deep, wrapping around his ribs like ivy.

He set the mug down and leaned forward, hands braced on the counter.

You left this town to get away from her; he reminded himself. *You don't get to come back and ruin what she's built.*

And yet — even as he said it, a part of him knew it was too late. Something had already cracked open the moment he saw her again.

By the time he finished his coffee, the ache in his chest hadn't eased. If anything, it had grown roots. Maybe it wasn't an obsession. Maybe it was hope—dangerous, foolish, impossible hope. Every corner of his kitchen seemed infused with her presence—the faint scent of vanilla, the echo of her laugh. He pressed his palms to the counter again, feeling both grounded and haunted, caught between the life he knew and the pull he could no longer resist. But for the first time in years, Noah Carter wasn't running from what he wanted.

Chapter 13

Lessons in Letting Go

By midmorning, the skies over Maplewood had turned the color of bruised plums. The air was thick and restless, like it was holding its breath before something broke.

Emma Lawson had been up since dawn, frosting maple scones and checking her phone every five minutes for weather updates. The news was grim: torrential rain, high winds, possible flooding. Just in time for the busiest weekend before Thanksgiving.

The bakery windows rattled as thunder rolled across the hills. The scent of the rain-soaked earth drifted through the cracked window, mingling with the warm sweetness of half baked pastries. Emma's stomach tightened. Every clap of thunder made walls vibrate and her nerves fray; she wished she could control the weather as easily as she controlled her ovens.

Hazel rushed in from the back, clutching a tray of muffins like a life raft. "Power's going in and out," she panted. "Half the town's already dark. Diner's still hanging on, though."

Emma's stomach sank. "Perfect. Just what I needed."

As if summoned by sarcasm, the lights blinked twice—then went out completely. The soft hum of the ovens died, leaving behind the hollow silence of defeat. The smell of half-baked pastries hung in the air, warm and taunting.

Hazel exhaled dramatically. "Well, there goes the day."

Emma pressed a hand to her forehead and forced herself to stay calm. *Grandma Lawson didn't raise quitters.* "We still have the generator," she said. "We'll plug in the mixers and one oven—just enough to finish the contest pies."

Hazel looked relieved. "You think we're the only ones who thought ahead?"

"Knowing this town?" Emma said dryly. "Absolutely."

She was half right.

By noon, rain pelted Maplewood in sheets, turning Main Street into a river. The bakery's lights flickered back to life thanks to the hum of her old generator out back. But before she could celebrate, the front bell jingled.

Noah Carter stepped inside, rain dripping from his hair, a scowl on his handsome, soaked face.

"Lawson," he greeted, voice rough with weather and irritation. "We need to talk."

Emma arched her brow. "You look like a drowned lumberjack."

He ran a hand through his hair, sending droplets flying. "Power's out at the diner. Storm fried my backup. I need your generator."

Hazel muttered under her breath, "Oh, this is going to be good."

Emma leaned against the counter, folding her arms. "My generator? The one currently saving all my contest pies?" Her pulse jumped as she looked at him. The rain clinging to his shirt made him look rough and wild, and for the briefest moment, Emma wondered if the storm outside mirrored the one building in her chest.

"The same," he said, clearly trying not to sound desperate. "I've got half the town huddled in the diner. Kids, old folks, tourists who got stranded. I can't serve cold food and awful coffee—it'll turn into chaos."

She smirked, delighting in the shift of control. "So, let me get this straight. You, Noah Carter—Maplewood's golden boy, the man who swears he can fix anything—came all the way here to ask me for help?"

His jaw ticked. "Don't make it sound like a marriage proposal."

Hazel choked on a laugh.

Emma took a slow step forward, savoring the moment. "Funny, though—you didn't seem to need my help when you left town without saying goodbye."

His lips curved, with a flash of mischief in his eyes. "You've been waiting years to throw that one, huh?"

"Maybe," she said sweetly. "Feels nice."

He exhaled. "Look, Lawson. I'm not asking for much. Just a loan. I'll bring it back once the storm passes."

She tilted her head. "And how do I know you're not just trying to sneak a look at my recipes? My contest bakes are in progress, and I know how competitive you can get."

His brows lifted, a grin tugging at his mouth. "You think I'd brave a monsoon to spy on your secret pie crust?"

She shrugged. "Wouldn't put it past you. You've always been a sore loser."

That earned a low laugh from him, the kind that curled heat low in her stomach. "Maybe I just remember what it feels like to lose *to you.*"

The way he said it—slow, deliberate—sent a ripple of electricity between them. Hazel, sensing where this was heading, grabbed her coat. "I'm just gonna… go check the back. You two have fun."

Neither of them looked away as she slipped out.

"Lawson," he said finally, stepping closer. "People are counting on me. You've got the only working generator in town."

"And I've got a contest to win," she countered, matching his stare. "So what's your offer?"

He leaned against the counter, dripping rain, looking infuriatingly unbothered. "You come to bake at the diner. Bring your supplies; bring the generator. We share the space. I'll keep your food warm; you keep the town fed. Everyone wins."

Her heart thudded. "And what makes you think I'd agree to that?"

"Because you care," he hissed. "And because, deep down, you miss the thrill of beating me to the punch."

Her pulse fluttered. "You're impossible."

"Persistent," he corrected, eyes glinting. "And you're blushing."

She snorted. "That's steam, not blush. Happens when the air's full of hot air—yours, specifically."

He laughed. "Still feisty. I missed that."

The last line hung between them, heavier than thunder. For a moment, neither moved. The storm outside roared, lightning flashing through the windows.

Finally, Emma broke the silence. "Fine. You can use my generator — if we share the kitchen. My rules, my bakes, no peeking."

His grin spread, slow and wicked. "Scout's honor."

"Pretty sure you got kicked out of scouts," she muttered.

He chuckled. "Yeah, for sneaking extra marshmallows. Some things never change."

By evening, they'd hauled the generator to the diner, strung extension cords through puddles, and powered the lights and ovens. The place was buzzing—neighbors taking shelter, laughter and worry mixing in equal parts.

Emma set up on one side of the kitchen while Noah flipped pancakes on the other, their movements an uneasy dance.

Every time she reached for flour, he was there, brushing past her shoulder. Every time he leaned down to grab a pan, his arm grazed her waist. Each brush against her sent a flicker of warmth up her spine, a reminder that proximity to him was more than physical-it was an ache she hadn't expected to feel again.

"Careful," she warned. "You're crowding my space."

"Your space?" he teased. "I'm pretty sure I paid the property taxes here."

Pumpkin Pie & Piercing Hearts

She rolled her eyes. "You're insufferable."

He leaned close, voice an inaudible murmur. "And yet, here you are, sharing your generator with me." Heat pooled low in her belly, and she felt her fingers linger on the counter just a fraction too long, aware of the faint scent of his cologne, the steady thrum of his heartbeat in the quiet moments between the thunder.

Her hands faltered, just slightly, as their eyes met.

Hazel's voice called from the front, "Do I need to install a mistletoe back there, or are you two managing fine?"

Emma's cheeks burned. "We're managing!"

Noah's grin was pure sin. "Barely."

The power hummed steadily, the storm outside still wild but distant now. As the night deepened, they worked side by side—flour-dusted, tired, and silently aware that something between them was shifting again.

When the generator sputtered for a heartbeat, the lights dimmed, and Emma's pulse raced.

He turned toward her, face half-lit, half-shadowed. "Guess we'll have to make sure the heat stays on," he breathed.

She met his gaze, refusing to back down this time. "Don't worry, Carter. Between the two of us, I think we've got enough heat to last all night."

He smiled slowly, as if someone had just dared him. "We'll see about that."

Thunder cracked—loud enough to shake the windows. Then, suddenly, everything went dark.

The hum of the generator stuttered once... then died completely.

For a heartbeat, the world went still. The only sound was the rain hammering against the glass, the storm wrapping Maplewood in velvet darkness.

Emma froze, her breath catching as the soft glow from the diner's front candles barely reached them. Every heartbeat seemed magnified in the darkness. She could feel the warmth radiating off him, smell the rain in his hair, and the space between them felt electric, charged with unspoken desire.

"Noah?" she whispered.

"Right here," came his voice—low, close, too close.

Her heart skipped. "You'd better not be using this blackout as an excuse to snoop around my pies."

"I'm not interested in your pies right now," he murmured, stepping closer until she could feel the heat of him, even through the cool air.

"Then what *are* you interested in?" She asked, pulse pounding.

He hesitated just long enough for her breath to hitch. "Guess you'll have to wait for the lights to find out."

Lightning flashed, flooding the room in stark white for a split second—just long enough for her to see him standing inches away, his expression unreadable, eyes dark with something that looked far too much like want. The flash left a ghost of heat lingering on her skin. Her pulse raced, her breaths shallow. She realized how dangerously aware she was of him-every nerve taut, every sense sharpened by the storm and the proximity of someone she still wanted, still feared.

The lights flickered back to life, humming low. Neither of them moved.

Flour dusted his forearm. Her hair was falling out of its braid, lips parted, heartbeat wild.

"Generator's back," she whispered, forcing a smirk. "Guess you didn't need your heat, after all," she said.

He grinned, slow and knowing. "Maybe not this time."

Their eyes locked, and in that tiny space between banter and silence, something shifted.

Something dangerous.

Something inevitable.

The storm outside roared again, wind howling down the street as if echoing what neither of them dared to say out loud.

Emma swallowed hard, turning back to her pie crust with shaking hands. But she could still feel his gaze on her—steady, unrelenting—like a promise waiting to be broken. She shocked her head, forcing herself to focus on the dough, but even the tactile feel of flour couldn't erase the awareness of him. He was there-every glance, every subtle shift in stance, telling her that the storm wasn't the only thing threatening to sweep her off her feet.

Chapter 14

A Kiss in the Candlelight

The storm had been raging for hours, hammering Maplewood with sheets of rain that streaked the diner windows and rattled the shutters. Inside, the hum of the generator mixed with the inaudible murmur of townspeople huddled in booths, wrapped in blankets and sipping cocoa. The air smelled of cinnamon, wet leaves, and sizzling bacon—a chaotic comfort that made the diner feel both alive and private at the same time. The generator had been humming for hours, powering ovens, lights, and the anxious chatter of townsfolk. Emma had barely slept, and the storm felt endless. Yet, somehow, having Noah here made the chaos feel personal, magnetic, and impossible to ignore.

Emma Lawson wiped her hands on her apron, glancing across the narrow kitchen space at Noah Carter. Noah had rolled up his sleeves, with damp hair stuck to his forehead, and his eyes locked on her with the same smoldering intensity she had felt since the generator had flickered back to life last night.

"You know," she said, rolling the dough out for the tenth time, "I'm not sure how much longer I can tolerate working next to you."

"No, I think you'll manage," he replied, leaning casually against the counter with that infuriating half-smile, "especially since you're the one inching closer every time I pass."

Emma rolled her eyes, though her pulse betrayed her. "Pass. Not an inch."

He laughed low and warm; the sound curling around her chest. "Oh, Lawson. You know better than anyone: inches count."

Hazel, stationed at the front counter to make sure none of the townsfolk got into mischief, rolled her eyes and whispered over her shoulder, "Someone get a fire extinguisher before these sparks burn the place down."

Emma shot her a sharp glare, but couldn't hide the tug of a smile. "We're fine," she muttered, though she was far from fine.

The baking continued, and soon playful chaos erupted. Noah reached for the same bag of flour she had, and a tiny cloud puffed into the air. "Hey!" she exclaimed, laughing. "Watch it!"

"Or what?" he teased, grinning like a boy half her age. He flicked a small pinch of flour toward her, and it landed on her nose.

Emma gasped, laughing so hard she almost dropped the rolling pin. "I'll get you back for that!" She swiped a handful and flicked it toward him.

The flour fight escalated quickly—hands brushing, fingers smudging sugar and dough, their laughter echoing against the walls. Each accidental touch left a jolt of heat in her chest. Each shared glance lingered a beat too long. She realized how easily he could throw her off balance, how every smirk, every careless brush of a hand, made her forget the hours of preparation, the storm, the contest-everything except him.

"Careful," he murmured, leaning closer than necessary, the scent of his rain-damp jacket wrapping around her. "You're crowding my space."

"You're crowding *me*," she shot back, though her voice wavered.

He leaned in, so close that she could feel his breath. "I like this kitchen," he whispered, voice low, teasing, and something deeper underneath. "Especially when you're in it."

Her pulse jumped. "I—"

He pressed his hand lightly on the counter near hers, blocking her movement. The electricity between them was thick enough to taste.

And then, just like that, everything happened in a single, impossible moment.

He dipped his head, and the laughter faded from her lips as his mouth met hers.

It was desperate, pent-up, and fierce—the culmination of months of stolen glances, unspoken attraction, and the restless dreams that had haunted both of them. Her hands flew to his chest, brushing against damp fabric and muscle, feeling the warmth and strength she had imagined so many nights. It was a culmination of months of stolen moments, of imagined touches in the quiet of her bakery, of wondering if he'd ever come back. The kiss was fierce and desperate-but underneath it, a fragile hope trembled, one that neither of them fully admitted aloud.

Noah's arms wrapped around her waist, holding her close but careful, as though letting go would shatter the fragile reality of the moment. Her hands tangled in his hair as the kiss deepened, and the world outside—the storm, the townspeople, the diner—faded into background noise.

It was a kiss full of laughter, longing, and the ache of years spent denying what had always been there. Every touch, every press of lips, every shared breath sent heat through her; she had no intention of controlling.

And then—a small, familiar voice pierced the charged haze.

Hazel's voice rang out, sharp and amused. "Emma! Noah! Somebody is *actually* about to throw a chair!"

They jolted apart. Emma's cheeks flamed, and Noah's grin faltered—but only slightly. Hazel pushed through the swinging door, eyes twinkling. "And I *just* walked in on you two smooching?" Emma wished she could disappear into the dough on the counter. Noah, for his part, didn't break eye contact as if daring her to scold him-but the brief flicker of amusement in his eyes betrayed that he too felt the awkward intensity of being caught.

Emma groaned, pulling flour from her hair. "Hazel! This is ridiculous!"

"Noah, you're supposed to be helping me with—oh, never mind," Hazel said, pointing toward the commotion in the diner. "Go save whoever's about to fight, but—by the way—what was *that*?" She wagged a finger, teasing. "You two better not think I didn't see that kiss. I saw it. Don't even deny it."

Noah leaned casually against the counter, hand still dangerously close to Emma's. "We were… just testing the recipe," he said, smirking.

Emma rolled her eyes, cheeks still flushed. "Sure. Testing the recipe."

Noah chuckled under his breath, brushing a strand of wet hair from his forehead. "Apparently, the hero part of me includes saving a couple of blushing bakers from embarrassment," he said, smirking at Hazel.

Hazel rolled her eyes but gestured to the diner. "Yeah, and someone needs to actually prevent a fight before the Johnson twins take each other out. Come on, Carter."

Noah strode to the front, calm and commanding. Two young men were posturing, fists raised over a spilled drink. His voice rang out over the storm's roar: "Alright! That's enough. Step back."

The men froze. Noah placed a hand lightly on each of their shoulders. "I don't want to hurt anyone tonight. Take a breath. If you want to fight, you can go outside and join the storm; otherwise, settle down. Everyone's fine. Problem solved."

Hazel smirked at him. "See? He is always the hero."

"Someone has to keep the peace," he said, brushing off his hands as if it were nothing. Then, leaning in slightly, he added under his breath in a teasing tone, "But it's a lot less stressful when I get to come back here."

He gave Hazel a wink, and she laughed, shaking her head before returning to smooth over the rest of the chaos.

Noah retreated to the back kitchen, finding Emma wiping flour off the counter, her cheeks still flushed from earlier. He leaned against the doorway, arms crossed, a crooked grin playing on his lips.

"You're back," she said, trying to sound composed but failing.

Tanisha Pollard

"Of course," he said, voice low and teasing. "Someone had to stop a fight, and now I get to come back to *my* favorite distraction."

Emma's stomach flipped. "My... distraction?"

"You heard me," he murmured, stepping closer, letting the space between them shrink just enough that her pulse jumped. "And don't even think about pretending you're not thrilled to see me."

She rolled her eyes but couldn't hide the smile tugging at her lips. "I'm... totally thrilled," she said, voice clipped.

Noah leaned closer, just enough for Emma to feel the warmth radiating from him. "You know," he murmured, voice low and husky, "we really should finish that flour fight... or start another."

Emma's heart hammered. "Careful, Carter. I might not resist this time."

He smirked, slow and knowing, leaning in ever so slightly. "Good. Neither can I."

Emma's fingers brushed his as she reached for a rolling pin, and the contact sent a jolt of electricity straight through her. His eyes flicked to her lips, then back to her eyes, holding hers captive. Each touch felt loaded with weeks of unspoken words, years of frustration, and the dangerous possibility that they were circling something neither of them had fully named yet.

The kitchen felt smaller, hotter, alive with tension. Every shared glance, every subtle touch, every unspoken word lingered like the sweet spice in the air around them. Even the storm outside seemed to fade in comparison to the storm building between them.

Noah tilted his head, voice low and husky. "You know... one more inch, and I might just forget all about baking."

Emma's breath hitched, heart hammering. She tried to mask it with a smirk. "Oh, I'm *terribly* sorry," she said, teasing yet aware she could barely think straight.

He leaned closer, letting the warmth of his body press against hers, but he stopped just short of touching lips. "No need to apologize... just don't fight it."

Her fingers itched to reach for him, to bridge the final space, and his hand twitched slightly, betraying the restraint in his voice. The candlelight flickered across his face, highlighting the smirk tugging at his mouth and the intensity in his eyes. Flour-dusted counters, the soft hum of the generator, the faint scent of cinnamon—all of it paled against the heat that had nothing to do with baking.

And there they stayed, inches apart, the air thick with desire and unspoken need. Every shallow breath, every subtle brush of hands, every heartbeat was a countdown to a fire neither of them could yet fully start. For a fleeting second, Emma caught a shadow in his eyes-hesitation, maybe guilt, a history he hadn't shared. The teasing grin didn't mask it, and her stomach tightened with curiosity and caution in equal measure.

Noah's green eyes softened for the briefest moment, and Emma caught a glimpse of something behind the smirk—a shadow of hesitation, a weight he wasn't sharing.

"There's... a lot I didn't tell anyone," he murmured, almost to himself, voice low. "Things I left behind... things I can't fix." Emma's mind raced. What had he left behind? Why had he gone? For the first time in weeks, the playful tension faltered under the weight of real questions she didn't dare ask-but wanted answers to.

Emma's brows furrowed, pulse still racing from their closeness. "What do you mean?"

He shook his head slightly, a teasing half-smile tugging at his lips, but the guarded look in his eyes betrayed him. "Later," he said finally, voice low, teasing but carefully restrained. "I'll tell you later."

Emma's heart skipped, a mix of curiosity and frustration swirling in her chest. The storm outside raged on, but inside Noah's kitchen, the heat, tension, and unspoken promises pulsed stronger than any tempest. Flour dusted counters, candlelight flickered, and the charged air between them was a storm all its own—waiting, simmering, ready to ignite.

Chapter 15

Butter, Sugar & Heat

The storm outside had softened to a steady drizzle, but inside Noah's kitchen, the air still crackled with the heat from last night's near-kiss. Morning light had seeped through the clouds, pale and silver, catching on the flour-dusted counters. The storm had calmed, but its echo still hummed through the dripping eaves outside. It had been barely twelve hours since the power flickered back, though it already felt like another lifetime. Emma leaned against the counter, rolling pin in hand, fingers still dusted with flour, while Noah lingered just a few inches away, watching her with that mix of teasing and intensity she couldn't quite read.

"You know," he began, voice low, almost a whisper, "I've been avoiding this for a long time."

Emma's heart skipped. "Avoiding… what?"

His gaze dropped to the counter, and he ran a hand through his damp hair, shoulders tightening slightly. "Avoiding you. Avoiding this—us. His voice

116

faltered, rough around the edges. "Back then, it was easier to pretend you were just the girl who beat me at the county bake-off, not the woman who made me question everything I thought I wanted. I left Maplewood because I was exhausted. Not just from work, or life, or everything in between. I burned myself out. The diner was failing, my dad's health was getting worse, and I felt trapped between staying for everyone and leaving before I turned into him. I thought if I built something on my own, I'd come back stronger. I didn't know how to handle what I felt, what I wanted, or what I'd leave behind if I stayed."

Emma's hands froze on the dough. Her chest tightened, the words hitting harder than any storm outside. "You... left because of me?" she asked softly, voice barely audible.

"No," he said immediately, shaking his head. "Not because of you. Because of me. I was not ready; I couldn't. Facing myself, my mistakes, and my fears wasn't something I was ready for. I thought leaving would fix it, but it only made the years stretch longer."

Her heart ached at the confession, the vulnerability raw and unguarded. She took a tentative step closer, brushing her hand against his as she reached for a bowl of sugar. "I... I thought you didn't care," she admitted, voice catching. "I thought you just... left me behind without a second thought." Her words came out sharper than she intended, a confession wrapped in accusation. The nights she'd watched the diner lights go dark replayed in her mind, the silence that followed louder than any thunderstorm.

"No," he said again, eyes locking on hers. "I thought I was protecting you. Protecting us. But I see now... I was only protecting myself from failing, from hurting you more."

Emma swallowed hard, the tight knot of old insecurities unraveling. She looked down at her hands, still dusted with flour, still trembling. "I've spent so long trying not to want someone... trying not to let myself hope. And now you're here, and... I don't know how to do this. How to trust myself, or you." hope scared her more than storms ever could. It demanded faith, and she'd never been good at that-not since he left, not since the bakery became her armor.

Noah's fingers brushed hers deliberately as he reached for a stick of butter. He cut it and set it on the counter, eyes never leaving hers. "You don't have to trust me right away," he whispered. "Just...

trust that I'm here now. That I'm not running anymore." The steadiness in his tone cut through her hesitation. It wasn't a grand promise, just a small truth spoken in the quiet kitchen–something she could almost believe in.

Her heart pounded as the tension between them shifted from playful and flirty to deeply intimate, and she bit her lip. The kitchen smelled of butter, sugar, and vanilla—a sweetness that seemed to mirror the tentative hope blooming between them.

"Noah..." she started, hesitating, "I..."

He took her hand gently, pressing it against his chest. "Hey. We'll take it slow. Step by step. But I need you to know... leaving was never about you not being enough." His thumb brushed a steak of flour from her wrist, a simple touch that felt like an apology and a promise in one motion. "It was my not being ready enough."

Emma's eyes glistened with unshed tears, the walls she had built around her heart crumbling. She let herself lean just a little closer, feeling the warmth radiating from him, the steadiness in his voice, the certainty in his presence.

"You really burned out?" she whispered, almost a question, almost disbelief.

He chuckled softly, a sound that made her chest ache. "I burned out on pretending. On running. I thought I could just walk away from what I wanted most without facing it. And the funny part? I've wanted this... wanted you... since the moment I left."

Emma's breath hitched. Her hands trembled, not from the chill in the kitchen, but from the heat that pooled in her chest. "Since the moment you left..." she repeated, testing the words on her tongue, letting them sink in.

"Yes," he said, stepping just a little closer, his presence overwhelming and grounding all at once. "And now... I'm not leaving."

The words hung in the air, thick with unspoken promises. For a moment, they simply stood there, the storm outside reduced to a soft patter, the kitchen glowing with candlelight and the scent of their shared labor. Butter and sugar, heat and tension—it all wrapped around them like a cocoon.

Emma finally let herself look up at him fully, searching his eyes for truth. "Then... we figure it out. Together?" outside, a car splashed through the puddles on Main Street. Life in Maplewood was already resuming, but inside the diner kitchen, the time seemed to still for them-a pause before the next step.

He nodded, a slow, deliberate smile tugging at his lips. "Together."

And in that moment, with flour dusting the counters and the faint warmth of the oven behind them, something fragile but unbreakable formed—a bridge of trust, desire, and the promise that neither distance nor doubt could sever.

Chapter 16

The Contest Heats Up

By morning, the storm had passed, but the air inside the diner still hummed with leftover heat—from the ovens, from the adrenaline of the bake-off practice, and from the way Noah kept looking at her. Morning light filtered through the storm-streaked windows, catching on the flour dusted counter. Outside, the drizzle had softened to a gentle mist, giving maplewood a calm, washed-clean look after the chaos.

Emma Lawson stood at the counter, carefully piping whipped cream onto a line of miniature caramel pies. Her focus should've been on texture and presentation—but every time Noah's shoulder brushed hers, every time she caught the faint scent of coffee and vanilla on his shirt, her pulse stumbled.

"Careful," Noah murmured, leaning close enough that his breath stirred a loose strand of her hair. "You're putting too much cream on that one." He reached past her carefully, not just brushing but deliberately letting his hand linger near hers as he steadied the bowl. It wasn't accidental—it was a claim, subtle but unmissable.

She arched her brow, refusing to look up. "And you're too close to my space again."

He smirked. "You say that like it's a problem."

Her cheeks warmed despite her best efforts to seem composed. "Maybe it is."

"Then why aren't you moving?"

She froze for just a second—because he was right. She hadn't moved. Not an inch. Her chest fluttered at the realization. Somehow, being so close didn't feel threatening. It felt like a conversation in touches, and she wasn't sure if she was winning or losing.

He reached past her to grab the bowl of whipped cream, his arm brushing along her side, slow enough to make her breath catch. "Let me show you how it's done," he said, his voice dipping low, playful but edged with something rougher.

Emma crossed her arms, trying to keep her tone steady. "Oh, I'd love to see this master class in pastry technique."

Noah dipped his finger into the whipped cream—just the tip—and then turned toward her, eyes glittering with mischief. "See," he said, "it's about precision."

Before she could react, he touched the cream to the corner of her lip. "Like that."

Emma blinked, startled. "You did not just—"

He grinned, completely unapologetic. "What? Quality control."

She glared—but the way her pulse was racing ruined the effect. "You're insufferable."

"Am I?" he murmured, taking a slow step closer. "Because I think you like it."

Her retort died on her tongue when he lifted his thumb to her mouth, wiping away the cream—but his gaze lingered on her lips.

The air between them shifted. It wasn't just playful anymore—it was molten.

She swallowed, her voice barely above a whisper. "You shouldn't do that."

He tilted his head. "You mean this?" He dabbed another tiny bit of cream on her cheek.

Emma laughed softly, exasperated and flustered all at once. "You're ridiculous."

"Maybe," he said, his grin softening. "But you're smiling again."

Her breath hitched at that. She hadn't realized it—but she was smiling. And for a moment, all the walls she'd built—the fear, the overthinking, the what-ifs—started to crumble.

She dipped her finger into the bowl, eyes narrowing in challenge. "Turnabout's fair play, Carter." The cream fight became a quiet war, each swipe a negotiation, each smudge a message. For the first time in weeks, she felt entirely present, entirely herself, entirely caught between mischief and something deeper.

Before he could step back, she swiped the cream across his jaw.

He froze, looking at her with a spark of something that was equal parts surprise and want. Then, slowly, he licked the corner of his lip and said, "That's not fair. You missed a spot."

Her voice came out quieter than she intended. "Where?"

"Here." His finger brushed along his jaw where the cream had landed. "You're the one who made the mess—you fix it."

Emma's breath faltered. Her fingers trembled slightly as she reached up with a towel, meaning to wipe it off, but his hand caught hers halfway, holding her still.

"Or," he said, his voice rougher now, "you could use your way."

Her heart skipped, heat flooding her face and chest. "My way?"

He leaned in closer, so close she could feel his warmth, the steady thrum of his heartbeat in the quiet kitchen. "You know what I mean."

For a heartbeat, neither of them moved. The moment stretched, taut and fragile, like spun sugar ready to snap.

Then Emma laughed softly, the sound breaking the tension but not diffusing it completely. "You're impossible."

"Persistent," he corrected.

Their eyes met, and she realized just how close they were standing—how natural it suddenly felt to be this near, to have him watching her like she was something worth savoring.

She turned back to the counter, trying to steady her voice. "If you keep distracting me, we'll never get these pies done before the judges show up tomorrow."

"Maybe distraction's part of my strategy."

"Oh, is that what you call sabotage now?"

He chuckled, the low sound curling down her spine. "I call it teamwork."

Their laughter softened the air again, and as they worked side by side, fingers brushing, sharing quiet glances, something inside Emma shifted. The kitchen no longer felt like neutral ground—it felt like theirs.

And for the first time in years, she wasn't just baking to win.
 She was baking *with someone who saw her.*

Noah's smirk lingered as he turned back to the oven, sliding in the last tray of pies. The soft *click* of the door shutting echoed in the quiet space. For a moment, all that filled the air was the hum of the mixer and the faint storm-drizzle outside.

Emma tried to focus on cleaning up the counter, but her hands were still trembling. Her heartbeat hadn't slowed since he'd said *"use your way."*

She felt him behind her before she heard him—his presence filled the room like a change in pressure. He reached around her to grab the towel she'd abandoned, his hand brushing her waist in the process.

Her breath hitched.

"You missed a spot," he murmured, his voice barely audible over the hum of the appliances.

"Where?" she whispered, even though she didn't really want to know the answer.

He pointed to her cheek—where a faint smear of cream still lingered. But he didn't move to wipe it off. He just smiled, slow and infuriatingly tender, and stepped back.

"Got it," she said quickly, wiping her cheek with the back of her hand.

"Sure you did," he teased, turning away before she could think of a comeback.

And that's when Hazel burst through the swinging door like a gust of chaos.

"Okay," she announced, hands on her hips, eyes darting between the two of them. "Which one of you geniuses left a trail of whipped cream leading *out of the kitchen*? Half the town's kids are trying to lick it off the counter like a dessert treasure hunt."

Emma froze, mortified. Noah tried—and failed—to stifle a laugh. Emma's mortification mingled with relief—Hazel's timing was impeccable, saving them from getting swept entirely into the moment. But the heat lingering in the room refused to dissipate; it had set something alight neither of them could yet name.

"Oh, you think this is funny?" Hazel shot back, eyes narrowing in mock accusation. "Because it looks like the two of you were having your *own* little taste test in here."

Emma's face went scarlet. "Hazel—"

"Don't even bother," Hazel interrupted, waving a hand dramatically. "I saw the look on your face when I walked in. I know what that look means."

Noah leaned on the counter, completely unbothered. "And what look is that?"

Hazel grinned like the cat that got the cream. "The I just realized my rival might actually taste better than pie look."

Emma groaned. "Hazel!"

The entire diner seemed to laugh with Hazel as she disappeared back through the door, still muttering about cream trails and "bakers behaving badly."

When the door swung shut again, the silence returned—but now it was thick with something unspoken.

Noah turned toward Emma, the teasing grin still playing at his lips. "You heard her," he said softly. "You've got a look."

Emma exhaled, her pulse fluttering in her throat. "You're impossible."

"And yet," he said, stepping closer, "you're still here."

Her breath hitched as his fingers brushed a strand of hair behind her ear, his touch lingering for just a moment too long.

"Maybe," she murmured, meeting his eyes, "I'm just waiting to see what happens next."

Noah smiled, slow and deliberate, his gaze dropping to her lips before flicking back up again. "Then I guess we'll both have to find out."

The air between them shimmered with something more than heat now—something fragile, hopeful, and far too dangerous to name.

Outside, thunder rumbled in the distance. Inside, the timer on the oven beeped, breaking the spell.

But as they pulled the pies from the heat, neither of them could quite shake the feeling that something else—something far sweeter and far riskier—had already started to rise between them.

When the last pie cooled and the laughter faded, neither of them made a move to leave. The diner was quiet again, emptied of the storm's chaos and Hazel's meddling, but the air still pulsed with everything left unsaid. Emma wiped down the counter in slow, distracted strokes, while Noah lingered by the door, pretending to check the locks. Every stolen glance, every almost-touch felt heavier now—like the space between them wasn't air at all, but gravity.

Outside, the clouds broke just enough for moonlight to spill through the rain-streaked windows, washing the kitchen in soft silver. It made the sugar on the counter sparkle. It made Noah look like something she might dream up.

And when their eyes met one last time, neither of them smiled. They didn't need to. The air between them promised what was coming next—something wild, inevitable, and just dangerous enough to make it worth the fall. Emma exhaled slowly, letting the quiet stretch around her. She wasn't rushing, but she wasn't turning away either.

Noah stayed close, his presence a steady pull, the promise of everything unspoken wrapped around them like the last tendrils of steam from the oven. Outside, the moon peeked through the clouds, casting silver light over the diner—a quiet witness to the storm that had just passed and the one that was only just beginning between them.

Chapter 17

What We're Really Competing For

The afternoon sun slanted through the bakery windows, casting long golden streaks across the counters. The storm's dampness lingered faintly in the air, mingling with the sweet scents of cinnamon and vanilla—a cozy, intoxicating comfort, almost enough to make Emma forget herself. Almost.

She moved around the counters with deliberate precision, but her hands betrayed her. Every time she reached for a mixing bowl, her gaze flicked to Noah. He was standing near the oven, arms crossed, leaning just enough to look casual—but his smoldering intensity made it impossible for her to concentrate.

"You know," he said, voice low, teasing, "I could just watch you all day and still call it practice."

Emma rolled her eyes, but the flush creeping up her neck told the truth her mouth wouldn't. "You would be bored in five minutes," she retorted, though her hands shook slightly as she whisked the batter.

He stepped closer, letting his hand hover near hers as he reached for the same bowl, a calculated closeness that made her chest tighten. Every inch of space between them seemed charged, every shared breath deliberate.

"You're shaking," he murmured, fingers grazing her hand as he handed her the whisk. "Or is that just excitement?"

Emma wanted to glare. She wanted to push him away. She wanted to kiss him all at once and never stop. Instead, she inhaled deeply, trying to steady herself. Her hands trembled, betraying the battle between desire and caution waging inside her.

Instead, she inhaled, trying to focus on the batter. "It's just… concentration," she muttered.

He leaned down, close enough that his lips nearly brushed her ear. "Right. Concentration." His voice dropped, a husky undertone that made her stomach tighten. "I can feel it."

Her breath hitched. She couldn't tell if it was the closeness, the smell of his rain-damp jacket, or the memory of all the stolen glances and restless nights she'd spent dreaming about him.

And then he smiled a slow, impossible smile. One she recognized from years ago—and one that still made her weak.

Before she could think, he closed the small space between them. His lips met hers.

His lips met hers with a force of longing and restraint—months of stolen glances, restless nights, and unspoken words culminating in this one impossible moment. Her hands rested lightly on his chest, testing the warmth, the solidity, the reality of him.

She whimpered softly, and that was all it took to push him over the edge of restraint. His lips deepened the kiss, fingers threading into her hair, thumb brushing over her jaw. He wanted to touch her everywhere, to let her know how long he'd waited, how much he'd missed her.

It was overwhelming. Her knees threatened to buckle under the intensity, and her chest ached from the rapid heartbeat that seemed to echo in her ears. Every part of her screamed to give in, to let the desire win.

But fear was stronger. She pulled away, pressing her hands against his chest to create space, heart racing and mind spinning.

"Noah... I... I can't," she whispered. The ache of wanting him clashed with the caution that had kept her safe for so long.

He froze, eyes dark and searching, as if trying to read the conflict etched across her face. "Emma..." His voice was low, rough, full of the same restrained fire she felt pooling in her stomach. "Why not?"

She shook her head, fighting back the wave of want threatening to consume her. "It's... too soon. We—this... we shouldn't..."

Noah's hand lingered at her waist, not moving away. The heat of him pressed into her, and her pulse pounded in response. He was patient, desperate, and devastating all at once.

"I know," he murmured. "I know it's too much." His thumb brushed a trembling strand of hair from her face. "But that doesn't stop me from wanting it. Wanting you."

Her chest heaved. Her resolve trembled. She wanted him more than she could admit, more than she'd allowed herself to feel for years.

And for a suspended heartbeat, they just stared at each other—flour-dusted, sweat-lightened, hearts thundering, aware of everything that could happen if they gave in… and everything they'd have to fight to resist.

The bakery was quiet around them, the golden light falling in streaks across counters and tiled floors. Outside, Maplewood basked in the calm after last night's storm, but inside, the tension between Emma and Noah promised a storm all its own—unrelenting, consuming, and inevitable.

Even with her pulling back, the warmth of her hands on his chest lingered like fire. He could feel the tremor in her body, subtle but undeniable, and it set every nerve in his body alight. Every inch of restraint he'd clung to vanished the second she leaned toward him, then broke away.

He reached out, brushing his fingers along her forearm, just enough to let her know he wasn't letting go. The brush was electric—soft, tantalizing, and utterly unignorable. He wanted to taste every inch of her, memorize the feel of her skin against his, the way her breath hitched when he moved closer.

"You're impossible," he murmured, voice low, almost a growl. "You've always been impossible."

Her lips twitched with a near-smile, her eyes softening even as panic lingered. "And you're infuriating," she shot back, voice trembling slightly. "Why does it always have to be you?"

He leaned closer, letting the faint heat of his body ghost along hers. "Because it's always been me," he whispered, teeth grazing the shell of her ear. "And now... it's now."

***

Her pulse thundered in her temples. The way he leaned into her, the way his fingers lingered on her arms and back, made it impossible to think rationally. Every rational thought — *contest, town, responsibilities* — crumbled like a dry pie crust under the pressure of his presence.

She wanted to give in, to let herself melt into him right there in the bakery. Her hands twitched toward him instinctively, aching to press into the warmth of his chest, to let her lips roam freely across the trail of heat he'd left on her skin.

And yet... fear clamped down on her heart like a vice. Years of caution, heartbreak, and habit didn't vanish in one kiss, no matter how right it felt. She pulled back just enough to create space, hands pressing lightly against his chest, feeling his heartbeat under her palms.

"I can't," she whispered again, voice barely audible over the flutter of her own breathing.

Noah's fingers lingered at her waist, reluctant to move. He leaned closer — daring, patient, and desperate all at once. "Then I'll wait," he whispered. "But don't think for a second this changes how I feel."

Her eyes dropped, chest rising and falling erratically. She wanted to argue, wanted to push him away, wanted to run. And yet, every fiber of her body ached to stay, to let herself feel what she'd denied for so long.

He studied her face — the flush creeping across her cheeks, the slight tremor in her lips, the way her eyes darted away—but not too far. She wanted this, even though she was terrified.

He let his fingers trail lightly along her arms, careful, teasing, letting her know he wasn't letting go—but also that he would wait. "Then I'll wait," he murmured. "But know this—my feelings haven't changed."

She swallowed hard, fighting a shiver. "I… I don't know what I am right now," she admitted, voice raw, honest. "I shouldn't feel this way."

"Good," he teased, pressing just a fingertip along her jaw. "Because you do."

Her breath hitched, and for one suspended heartbeat, they simply stood there, hands brushing, hearts hammering, flour-scented warmth enveloping them. Time slowed. She heightened every sense—the soft hum of the oven, the golden streaks of light across the counters, the faint sweetness of sugar in the air—and yet, none of it mattered except the ache between them.

Emma's chest rose and plummeted. "I have to…" she started, but the words faltered.

Noah caught her hand in his again, holding it gently but firmly. "I know," he whispered, as though he could feel every conflict warring inside her. "And I won't make you do anything you're not ready for."

She closed her eyes briefly, let out a shaky breath, and stepped back finally, creating enough space to breathe and think. Her pulse still screamed, her body still tingled, and her mind swam, knowing that everything had just shifted.

He let her go—but his eyes never left hers. "Emma," he murmured, voice low and restrained. "This isn't the end. You know it's not."

Her lips pressed into a thin line, heart pounding, knowing he was right. And somewhere deep inside, beneath the fear and the uncertainty, she wanted him to be right.

Outside, the sun dipped low, bathing the bakery in warm amber light. Inside, the air thrummed with unspoken words and restrained desire. Neither had crossed the final line, but both knew it was only a matter of time before the storm they'd held at bay finally broke.

Chapter 18

Burnt Edges, Soft Centers

Emma sat at the small table in her bakery, hands wrapped around a steaming mug of cocoa, letting the warmth seep into her chilled fingers. Outside, the town hummed with the quiet rhythm of late November afternoon, leaves skittering across the streets in the autumn wind, a reminder that the contest was only days away. Inside, however, her mind was a storm.

Her thoughts refused to settle. Noah's kiss—the heat, the taste, the intensity—replayed over and over. She'd pulled back, told herself she was protecting her heart, but each memory made her pulse spike anew. *Why did it feel so right? So impossibly familiar? Like a place she'd been waiting to return to without realizing it.*

Hazel appeared in the doorway, arms crossed, a sly smile tugging at her lips. "You've been staring at that cocoa for ten minutes like it's going to give you answers," she said, sliding into the chair across from Emma.

Emma flushed, not bothering to hide it. "I'm... thinking," she murmured, eyes fixed on the mug.

Hazel leaned forward, voice gentle but insistent. "Thinking or overthinking?"

Emma opened her mouth to protest, but no words came. Hazel sighed, tapping her finger against the table. "Emma, you've built walls higher than the bakery shelves. And it's not just the contest you're afraid of losing—it's him."

Her heart skipped. She looked up, meeting Hazel's gaze. "I'm not—"

"Stop lying to yourself," Hazel interrupted, eyes twinkling with both amusement and exasperation. "You're terrified, yes. But it's not about the contest. It's about him. Noah. Carter. The one who left town and somehow still managed to be the most infuriatingly distracting man alive."

Emma clenched her mug tighter, trying to force herself to look away. "He left. I didn't. That's the whole point."

"Exactly," Hazel said, leaning back and tilting her head. "You've been carrying this like a burnt crust—hard and defensive on the outside—but you're soft in the middle. You can't ignore that heat he brings just because you're scared of getting burned." "And remember," Hazel added, tapping the table for emphasis, "the contest is ticking closer every day. You can't let fear steal this—him or your chance to shine."

Emma's chest ached, part frustration, part longing. "It's... complicated. He's... he's everything I didn't know I wanted but can't have."

Hazel smirked knowingly. "Everything you didn't know you wanted is exactly why you're scared. Because what if you finally let yourself feel it and it goes up in flames? You think you can't handle that."

Emma bit her lip, realizing Hazel was right. Every instinct in her had been screaming to pull back, to overthink, to keep her emotions locked up tight. And yet... her body remembered, her mind remembered, and her heart refused to forget Noah's kiss.

Hazel leaned closer, voice dropping to a whisper. "Emma, love isn't a perfectly baked pie. Sometimes the edges burn, sometimes it's messy, sometimes it's sticky—but that's what makes the center soft and worth it. You've got to stop pretending you don't want the heat."

Emma's fingers traced the rim of her mug, eyes downcast. "I... I just—"

"You're scared," Hazel finished for her. "And that's fine. But don't let fear ruin what's right in front of you. You've got a choice: let it go cold, or risk the burn for something real."

Emma exhaled slowly, the weight of Hazel's words pressing into her chest. For the first time in hours—or maybe days—she admitted to herself that yes, she did want him. That desire was messy, frightening, but undeniable. And yes, she was scared—but maybe she was ready to risk it.

But as she glanced toward the bakery counter where the sunlight hit the flour dust like gold, her mind wandered inevitably to Noah—how he'd pressed close, how his hands had lingered, how his eyes had searched hers for permission to cross the line she hadn't let him pass.

And despite the walls she had built, she knew one thing with terrifying clarity: she couldn't stop thinking about him.

Not anymore—not while the contest loomed, not while the days were slipping past, and certainly not while Noah was here, so close she could feel the pull of him in every thought.

Chapter 19

The Things Left Unsaid

Noah pushed open the diner's door, the familiar bell jingling overhead. The smell of fresh coffee, sizzling bacon, and warm bread hit him like a wave of memory, instantly grounding him. Maplewood felt smaller than he remembered, yet somehow more intimate, each corner of the diner steeped in nostalgia and whispers of the past—and a month's worth of memories crowded into these November days.

He leaned against the counter, scanning the room, and felt the familiar pang in his chest—seeing townspeople he'd grown up with, hearing the soft laughter and low chatter. His eyes caught the edge of the baking station, and for a moment, the present blurred.

His aunt stood beside him, flour dusting her apron, hands guiding him as he pressed dough into a pie pan. "Noah," she said gently, her voice soft but firm, "you can't just throw ingredients together and expect love to come out on its own. A pie—and a life—needs attention, patience, and care. You put love into it, and it comes back to you."

He had frowned at the time, frustrated that patience mattered more than speed. But her hands had guided him so carefully, and when he looked up, he saw her smile, warm and unwavering. "Watch," she said, brushing flour from his cheek, "the best pies—and the best people—are worth waiting for."

Even then, he hadn't fully understood. But now… the words struck him in the chest like a bell, echoing in the empty spaces his life had carried for years.

***

Back in the present, Noah set his coffee cup down with a soft clink, eyes distant. He'd been burned out, running from responsibilities and emotions alike. Leaving Maplewood had felt necessary then, a way to escape the pressure, the expectations, and the ache of wanting something—or someone—he wasn't ready to fight for.

But now, seeing Emma, watching her dedication in her bakery, feeling the pull that had never truly left, he realized he had been running from himself. Every whisk of sugar, every crust pressed with care, every pie she'd baked perfectly—it reminded him not only of his aunt's lessons but also of Emma herself: patient, passionate, and alive in a way he'd tried to ignore.

He remembered all the moments he had wanted her back then, all the times he had caught himself imagining a life with her. He had been too scared, too lost in his own chaos, and the town—small, familiar, comforting—had seemed like a cage and a sanctuary at the same time.

And yet... seeing her now, flour-dusted and beautiful, with that fire in her eyes that hadn't dimmed over the years, he knew he wanted more than fleeting moments. He wanted her.

Noah rubbed the back of his neck, tension coiling through him. The diner buzzed around him, oblivious to the storm of desire and regret inside him. Every laugh, every smile from a patron, every clatter of dishes reminded him of time lost—and time he couldn't get back.

148

Pumpkin Pie & Piercing Hearts

His hand drifted to the edge of the counter, brushing the spot where he had stood countless times with Emma in his memory, imagining the warmth of her body, the flash of mischief in her eyes, the softness of her lips when she had kissed him.

The ache of all the unsaid words, all the choices he hadn't made, filled his chest, heavy and bittersweet.

"Love isn't perfect," he whispered to himself, echoing his aunt's words. "But it's worth every risk, every heartbreak, every second of hesitation."

He glanced out the window toward Maplewood's quiet streets, thinking of Emma's laugh, her determination, and the way she had pushed him to feel again. He knew now: he wouldn't run. Not anymore. But proving himself, earning her trust... that was going to take more than words. More than charm. He had to show her he was worth the risk.

But he also knew that before he could have a chance with her, he had to find a way to prove it—not just with words, but with patience, effort, and the kind of love his aunt had always shown him through pies and gentle guidance.

Noah sat back against the counter, eyes softening, heart aching, and a small, hopeful smile tugging at his lips. "There's no time to waste," he thought.

"The month is almost gone, and every day counts-if I want her, if I want this, I have to act now, carefully, but without hesitation."

Chapter 20

Falling, Like Leaves

Maplewood's streets were painted gold and crimson as autumn leaned heavily on the town, leaves twirling in the crisp wind. Emma adjusted her scarf, trying to ignore the chill creeping through her coat—but it wasn't the weather making her shiver. November was already halfway gone, and the contest was looming, but this confrontation threatened to throw everything off balance.

Dean's car pulled up in the small parking lot outside the bakery, tires crunching over fallen leaves. Her stomach dropped the moment she saw him. Memories slammed into her all at once—the betrayal, the heartbreak she had tried to bury.

✱✱✱

The memory hit her like a punch. She could see it as clearly now as she had then: the dimly lit room at her best friend's apartment, the soft hum of music she'd once loved, the flicker of candlelight across the walls.

Dean had been charming—voice smooth, hands confident, eyes warm in the way that had made her heart flutter. He had leaned close, brushing a stray strand of hair from her cheek, whispering promises she wanted to believe: *"You're the only one I care about. I need you, Emma."*

She had believed him.

She remembered stepping out for a glass of water, only to hear muffled laughter that didn't belong to her. Curiosity nudged her toward the bedroom, and then the sight hit her: Dean, tangled in the sheets with *her best friend*, both laughing as if she didn't exist.

Time froze. Her stomach twisted. The betrayal was sharp, cutting deeper than anything she had ever felt. His gaze met hers for just a second—smug, unapologetic, cocky. No guilt. No hesitation. Just the casual cruelty of someone who didn't care what he destroyed.

Her knees buckled, hands gripping the doorframe to steady herself. Tears threatened, but anger roared louder. She had wanted to scream, to hit him, to make him feel even a fraction of the pain he had caused—but she had left instead, her pride and fury her only armor.

She had sworn she would never let him back into her life, never let him touch her heart again, never allow the soft, trusting part of her that had loved him to exist. And she had kept that promise—for years.

Even now, years later, the memory sent a shiver through her spine. The betrayal wasn't just about what he did—it was about the complete disregard for her feelings, the way he had treated her like an afterthought, a stepping stone for his own pleasure.

Emma's hands clenched around her scarf in the present, knuckles whitening. *I will never forgive him. Not now, not ever.*

✳✳✳

Back in the present, Dean pushed through the bakery doors, smirk firmly in place. "Emma Lawson," he said, voice smooth and venomous. "Still playing baker while the real world passes you by?"

Emma's hands clenched around a rolling pin she had been cleaning. "Dean... what are you doing here?" Memories of betrayal surged, her pulse spiking. Not just fear... anger. She wasn't the same person he'd left behind.

"No reason," he said, eyes scanning the bakery until they landed on her, sharp and calculating. "Just checking who's still pathetic enough to think pies are a career."

Noah, wiping down a counter nearby, felt heat spike through him. Every muscle coiled with protective instinct. The tension in the air snapped like a live wire.

Hazel appeared beside him, sensing the rising storm. "Oh no, he's here," she muttered under her breath. Her eyes scanned Dean, assessing the danger. "Emma, stay behind me if it comes to it."

Dean's smirk widened. "Still got friends to babysit you?" he mocked.

Noah didn't hesitate. He stepped forward, voice low and dangerous. "Emma's doing fine. You? You've already proven exactly who you are. And it's not welcome here." His eyes flicked to Emma for a split second, softening with concern, before snapping back to Dean. Every muscle in his body radiated a warning: cross this line, and you'll regret it.

Dean's gaze flicked to Noah, a challenge in his eyes. "Oh? And who are you exactly? The guy she's been daydreaming about?"

Noah's jaw tightened. "I'm the guy who doesn't let anyone talk to her like that," he said evenly, voice taut, full of warning. "You might want to leave. Now."

Emma's cheeks flushed—not with embarrassment, but with a mix of fear and gratitude. She had never seen Noah like this: controlled, but deadly serious.

Dean laughed, stepping closer. "Protective, huh? That's cute. Too bad she doesn't need it. You can't save her from reality."

Hazel crossed her arms, stepping between them. "Reality? You mean the reality of being a liar and a backstabber?" Her voice was sharp, cutting. "Emma doesn't need saving. She needs you out of her sight."

Noah's eyes never left Dean. "She doesn't need saving, but you? You need to leave."

Dean smirked but hesitated slightly, sensing the united front of Hazel and Noah. "This isn't over," he said, voice empty of warmth, before finally retreating toward the door, the crunch of leaves announcing his departure.

Emma exhaled shakily, turning to Noah and Hazel. "I… thank you both," she said, voice trembling.

Noah stepped closer, brushing a strand of hair from her face, thumb lingering on her cheek. "You don't have to thank me," he murmured. "I'll always stand up for you."

Hazel nudged her shoulder playfully. "And don't think you get to pretend that heat isn't there between you two," she teased, a mischievous glint in her eyes. "That kiss the other night? Don't deny it."

Emma's lips pressed into a thin line, cheeks burning. "Hazel!" she hissed, half embarrassed, half exasperated.

Noah's hand found hers, holding it gently but firmly. "You okay?" he asked, voice soft but laced with promise. Her heart skipped—not from fear this time, but from the undeniable warmth and safety she felt in his presence. November had brought storms, both outside and inside her heart, but this one felt different.

She nodded, fingers tightening around him. "Yes… thanks to both of you."

Outside, the autumn wind stirred the leaves like a soft applause. Inside, the bakery hummed with warmth, flour-scented air, and the heat of tension that refused to fade. Emma realized, with a mix of fear and anticipation, that Noah wasn't just there to protect her from Dean. He was there to stay. And she didn't want him to leave.

Chapter 21

The Storm Before the Feast

A soft drizzle fell against Emma's bakery windows after the storm had calmed slightly. It was only a day after Dean's unexpected visit, and though the town had quieted, the echo of that confrontation still clung to her like the smell of rain. The glow from the pendant lights bounced off the polished counters, casting warm golden reflections across the room. The aroma of cinnamon, nutmeg, and vanilla filled every corner, wrapping the space in a comfort that felt almost intimate. She inhaled deeply, letting the familiar scent soothe the nervous energy that had been building in her chest since the moment she'd seen Dean's face. But tonight, with Noah here, that weight felt lighter–different.

Noah leaned against the counter, watching Emma roll out her dough with practiced precision. The flour dusted her hair like snow, tiny particles catching the light as she moved. His pulse quickened at the sight, and he tried not to let his eyes linger too long—but it was impossible. He remembered the first time he'd seen her like this–focused, strong, entirely in her element–and how he'd been too proud, too scared to admit that she was the one person who ever made him feel grounded.

"You're getting better at that," he said, voice low, teasing. "I might actually have to admit defeat this time."

Emma smirked without looking at him. "Not a chance. I've been practicing in secret." "You still haven't beaten my pumpkin pie record," he teased, recalling their first playful competition. Her laugh this time sounded freer, softer–like the beginning of forgiveness. She flicked a small trail of flour toward him, which he caught with one hand, smirking. "Secret practice, huh? Sounds... suspicious."

"Suspicious? No, just... skilled," she replied, eyes sparkling with mischief.

"You know," he murmured, his voice low and smooth, "if I didn't know better, I'd think you were enjoying this—working beside me, I mean."

Emma shot him a sharp glance, flour dusting her cheeks. "Enjoying *you*? Never," she said, though the twitch of her lips betrayed her.

He grinned, stepping just close enough that their arms brushed as they reached for the same rolling pin. Heat shot up her spine at the contact. "Careful," he whispered, "we might get distracted."

"Distracted? By what?" she countered, trying to sound casual but failing. Her pulse thumped erratically in her ears.

"By you," he said simply, voice dropping, dark and warm. Her breath caught. The words hit a place she thought had long gone numb. She wanted to look away, to remind herself that he'd once left–but her heart, traitorous and hopeful, didn't listen.

Their movements grew smaller, closer—hands lightly grazing as they measured sugar, brushed whipped cream from each other's fingers, and tasted their handiwork from the same spoon. Every laugh, every playful swipe of flour, every teasing brush of hands sent sparks crackling between them. Every shared laugh and glance felt like stitching together something that had once been torn. She caught herself wanting to believe that maybe people could come back–not just to a place, but to each other.

Emma's chest rose faster as he leaned in to whisper something about "testing the consistency," but the closeness of his body, the warmth radiating from him, made her forget her words. The air smelled of vanilla, cinnamon, and him—an intoxicating combination that left her heady.

He brushed a hand over hers as she reached for the whisk, fingers lingering too long. "You know," he murmured, "you're impossible to resist, even when you try."

"Carter—" she began, heart racing, but he cut her off with a soft, teasing smile.

Noah leaned in, tucking a stray curl behind her ear. Emma blush his closeness getting to her. He whispered, "You drive me crazy. All I do is think about you all day long."

He nipped her ear, pulling a gasp out of her. Emma pulled away and continued to whisk the whipped cream.

Hours passed in a blur of sugar, laughter, and stolen touches. They talked about small things between tasks–the upcoming contest, the smell of burnt caramel, the townspeople's gossip–but beneath every word was the steady pulse of something unspoken. Every time their fingers brushed, silence said what words couldn't. Every so often, Noah would brush against her side, lean close enough that she could feel the warmth of his chest, and Emma would catch herself breathing shallowly, fingers trembling slightly.

"You know?" he began. "You never let me actually taste anything, and there's something in particular that I want to taste."

Emma blushed deep red. "Is it my amazing whipped cream?" She said he knew she was playing hard to get, but he was determined to push her further.

"You know what, yes, actually."

Noah pulled the bowl from her a little too roughly, sending the whisk clattering on the marble countertop. Some of the whipped cream fell on both of them. Emma gasped while Noah laughed. Some of the whipped cream had fallen on Emma's neck. Noah leaned in, whispering, "You're messy. Let me help you clean up." He then ran his wet tongue slowly up the side of her neck. Emma pushed her body into him as if begging him not to stop. He continued kissing her neck until she started whimpering.

Emma had had enough of the teasing. It was her turn to have fun. She didn't care about the whipped cream on his apron; she just wanted him, but she was going to make him beg for it. She leaned over and whispered, "That wasn't as hot as you'd like to think" then she nipped his earlobe and then walked away.

Pumpkin Pie & Piercing Hearts

The bakery clock ticked away the hours, unnoticed. Finally, Emma glanced toward the darkened windows and the soft patter of rain. "We… should probably head back," she muttered, cheeks flushed. "It's late, and I don't want to get soaked."

Noah caught her hand, thumb brushing over hers. "Yeah… I guess we should. But," he added with a smirk, "I'm not done with you yet."

They dashed through the drizzle, coats pulled tight, flour and whipped cream remnants on their hands and sleeves. Letting him follow her home felt like crossing an invisible line. She'd kept her word so small for so long–safe, predictable–vut Noah's laughter chasing her through the rain made her wonder if she'd been playing it too safe. Every step closer to her house was another beat of anticipation. By the time they reached her door, breathless from both haste and heat, the quiet of the night made the tension between them even more palpable.

Emma fumbled with her keys, heart hammering, as Noah leaned casually against the doorframe, smirk teasing, eyes dark and promising. "After you," he said, voice low, but the grin never left his face.

Inside, the warm glow of her living room greeted them. The soft hum of her old heater filled the quiet and the faint scent of vanilla candles mingled with rain. It felt lived-in, imperfect, but his presence made it feel whole. Emma kicked off her damp shoes, rolling up her sleeves nervously. Noah stepped closer, letting the door click shut behind them. The air between them felt heavier now, thick with the unspoken, the lingering heat, the sparks that had carried from the bakery.

Emma leaned against the bathroom sink, damp hair clinging to her neck, and crossed her arms. "I'm taking a shower," she said, trying to sound casual, though her pulse betrayed her. She needed a moment–not to escape him, but to steady the wild rhythm of her heart. Being near him stirred something she hadn't let herself feel in years: anticipation.

Noah leaned against the doorway, damp hair still sticking to his forehead, water dripping from the storm outside. "Just a shower?" he asked, voice low and teasing. "Or… are you inviting me in?"

Emma's eyes widened. "I—what?"

He smirked, stepping closer. "I didn't say I was just going to *stand here*." His gaze lingered on her, dark and knowing, sending a shiver down her spine.

"I'm… not sure that's a good idea," she murmured, but the twitch of her lips betrayed her.

"Oh, come on," he said, fingers brushing hers as she moved toward the shower. "It'll be fun."

Before she could argue further, he followed her into the warm cascade of water. Steam curled around them as he closed the gap, letting droplets fall between them, the scent of soap and wet hair mingling with the heat radiating from their bodies. The sound of the water filled the air, steady and calming. For a heartbeat, neither spoke. The tension between them wasn't just desire–it was history, apology, and the silent question of whether they could really start again.

"You're impossible," Emma muttered, gripping the shower rail for balance.

"Maybe," he said, voice husky, low enough to make her stomach flutter. "But I'm honest."

Their hands brushed, lingering longer than necessary. Fingers traced arms, shoulders, even the small curve of her back, and each touch left sparks in its wake. Emma's pulse raced; every accidental nudge of hips, every whisper in the steam-laden air, made her forget her earlier resistance.

"Careful," he murmured, leaning close enough that their chests almost touched. "I might not behave."

Emma swallowed, a shiver running down her spine. "Neither might I," she admitted, voice barely above a whisper.

Steam, heat, and tension coiled around them. The water ran over shoulders, arms, and legs as playful touches lingered, teasing glances became heated, and whispered words carried promise. The bakery, the rain, and the night outside seemed worlds away.

Finally, Emma took a breath and stepped back. "We... should finish this later," she said, voice shaking. He didn't push her. Instead, he simply nodded, eyes softening in a way that made her chest ache. It wasn't about what they could do–it was about what they might finally build together.

"Later?" Noah smirked, letting his wet hand brush hers as he handed her a towel. "I don't think we can wait."

Her cheeks flushed as she pulled the towel around herself, and he followed, wrapping a towel around his waist, his presence impossibly magnetic. "The bedroom is... more comfortable," she admitted, voice trembling slightly.

They moved together, dripping and flushed, from the bathroom to her bedroom. Every brush of hands, every accidental touch along the way, heightened the anticipation. The soft glow of her lamp, the crisp sheets, and the intimacy of the moment made her pulse hammer.

Finally, she sank onto the edge of her bed, breathless, heart racing. Noah leaned against the doorway, smirking teasing, voice low and dangerous. "So... now what?"

Emma leaned back, flushed and trembling, knowing exactly what *could* happen next. For the first time, she didn't feel afraid of what came next–only ready.

Noah took that as an invitation to join her, but he was going to make her beg him to fuck her mercilessly.

Noah walked over to the bed while Emma watched with anticipation. The bed dipped as he climbed over her. When he reached her mouth, he kissed her deeply. While their tongues battle for dominance, his hands explore her body, discovering she's wet. Breaking the kiss, he left light, feathered kisses on her neck, chest, and breasts. Roughly, he sucked each nipple, making her back arch. He continued to trail lower until he buried his face between her thighs. He ran his tongue through her slit and groaned. "Fuck you taste so good," he murmured. She moaned as he tortured her clit with fast flicks of his tongue. He tongued fucked her restlessly. She was about to come, and he was ready for every drop to be lapped up by him. She came so hard that she screamed his name so loud that it seemed to shake the walls.

Noah couldn't hold back anymore. He had wanted this for a long time. He positioned himself at her entrance and with one hard thrust he filled her to the hilt. Her back arched, he gave her body a second to adjust to his size. He started moving in her slowly at first, drawing out the pleasure, wanting this to last all night.

Pulling out of her, he commanded her, "Turn over now" She complied quickly, anticipating his next move. He lined himself up again this time, pushing inch by inch into her til he filled her completely. "Emma, baby, be a good girl and fuck me back."

Emma obeyed without hesitation. Noah gathered her hair in his hands, pulling roughly as he fucked her from the back. Emma was no angel; she played her part and pushed back into him, making her walls ripple from him hitting her in the spot that drove her crazy.

"Noah, I'm going to cum, please don't stop," Noah began thrusting faster in her. His hand went between them, and he pinched her clit hard, making her scream. He wasn't far behind her as her walls squeezed him. He couldn't hold on any longer. "Fuckkk Emma, Christ," he collapsed on her once he came. They lay there for a moment before he pulled out of her completely. Noah got up and went to the bathroom. He came back with a warm washcloth and cleaned her up. She winced a little, sore after their excursion. Finally, Noah came back to bed, and they fell asleep in a tangle of legs and cuddling.

Chapter 22

A Slice of Forgiveness

Sunlight streamed in through the curtains, highlighting the rumpled sheets and the aftermath of a night neither of them could forget. Emma stirred, heart hammering as consciousness fully hit. Her body still remembered the feel of Noah against her, and panic surged in full force.

"Oh no. Oh no, oh no…" she muttered, burying her face in the pillow. *What did we do?* Her pulse raced as memories of last night—the flour on their hands, the way he had joined her in the shower, the heat of their bodies pressed together—flashed through her mind.

Noah shifted beside her, stirring at the sound of her whispered panic. He opened his eyes slowly, dark and sleepless, scanning her face. There was that panicked flush in her cheeks, that tense line of her shoulders… and it hit him all at once.

"Emma…" His voice was low, steady, but there was a flicker of hurt she couldn't miss.

She bolted upright, pulling the blanket around her like a shield. "Noah... I—last night—I don't know if it was right! I mean, we... it was..." Words tumbled out in a rush, stammering, faltering, like she couldn't get them out fast enough.

He ran a hand through his hair, jaw tight. "Emma..." he started, then paused, swallowing the first spike of frustration. "Look... it wasn't a mistake. Not for me."

Her chest tightened, panic twisting into guilt. "But I—I don't know if I can—this is too much. I... I've never..." Her voice cracked as she buried her face in her hands.

Noah exhaled slowly, moving closer, placing a hand on her arm, warm and grounding. "Emma," he whispered, brushing a damp strand of hair from her forehead, "I get it. I'm not saying this is simple. I'm not saying it's easy. But last night... it was real. And I don't regret a second of it."

She peeked through her fingers, tears pricking her eyes. "I'm scared," she whispered. "Scared of feeling this... of losing myself, of... losing you."

He crouched slightly, tilting her chin up, his eyes locking onto hers with an intensity that made her breath catch. "You're not losing me," he murmured.

"You never had to worry about that. I'm right here. And if it scares you… then feel it. Feel it with me. Don't hide it. Don't hide from me."

Emma's chest heaved. His calm steadiness cut through the whirlwind of panic inside her, even as desire curled through her like fire. She wanted to argue, to retreat, but every inch of her wanted to **lean into him**.

"I don't want to mess this up," she whispered, trembling.

"Then don't think about it," he said, voice husky, lips twitching in a small, almost wicked grin. "Just… be here. With me."

Her pulse raced as the tension between them dissolved into something molten and electric. She laughed shakily, a small, breathless sound. "One slice at a time?"

"Exactly," he murmured, pressing a gentle kiss to her temple, lingering in a way that made her knees weak.

The air was thick with desire and relief, panic slowly melting into connection. Noah's hands traced her arms, her waist, lingering touches that left sparks in their wake. Emma felt herself melting

into him, the walls of fear crumbling with every
brush of skin, every whispered word, every shared
breath.

"Okay," she murmured, voice barely audible.
"Okay... I can do this. With you."

Noah's lips curved into a slow, victorious smile.
"Good," he whispered, voice low and husky,
"because I'm not letting go. Not now. Never."

Emma's pulse raced as she pressed against him,
their bodies tangled in the sheets, the morning
sunlight brushing their skin. Panic had melted into
heat, desire coiling tight and urgent between them.

Noah leaned close, voice low and husky, brushing a
damp curl from her face. "Good," he murmured,
lips near her ear, "because I'm hungry... for
breakfast."

Emma shivered, breath catching at the playful tone,
her chest rising and falling as he teased and trailed
kisses down her neck, hands tracing curves she had
only just let herself feel.

There was only heat, only them, only the tension
and the laughter that spilled between touches,
whispered words, and shared breath.

She grabbed her phone from the nightstand, fingers trembling slightly. "I should call Hazel," she murmured.

Noah's lips brushed her shoulder, teasing. "Go ahead... make it quick," he murmured, voice low and husky.

Emma dialed and held the phone to her ear. Hazel answered immediately, curiosity in her voice. "Emma? Are you coming into the bakery today?"

Emma swallowed hard. "No... not today," she said, voice breathless. "I... I'll be... staying home." She shot a quick glance at Noah, cheeks warming as he smirked.

From behind her, Noah's teasing voice rang out, "Yeah, she's *staying home*... with me!"

Emma groaned, covering the phone. "Noah!"

Hazel's laugh was sharp and amused. "Ohhhh... now it all makes sense. The bakery can wait, but breakfast with... him? That's priority number one, huh?"

Emma buried her face in the pillow, cheeks flaming. "Hazel! Don't—"

"Relax, Emma," Hazel said, still laughing. "I'll hold down the fort. You two enjoy… whatever it is you're doing at home."

Emma finally hung up, her heart hammering, and Noah's smirk widened as he brushed a hand down her arm. "See? Even Hazel knows you're mine today."

Her breath hitched, and before she could respond, his lips were on hers, teasing, tasting, exploring. The world narrowed—just him, her, and the heat that had been building for months.

Hours slipped by like minutes. Every touch, every whispered word, every playful tease drew them closer. They laughed, gasped, and tangled in the sheets until the world outside—the town, the bakery, the storm—completely faded.

Chapter 23

When the Oven Door Opens

The bell above the diner door jingled as Emma stepped inside, the comforting aroma of coffee, sizzling bacon, and warm bread wrapping around her like a familiar hug. It had been weeks since she'd been here, and though everything looked the same, it felt different. The memories of past mornings, and of Noah moving effortlessly behind the counter, tugged at her chest in ways she couldn't ignore. Morning sunlight slanted through the windows, casting golden streaks across the chrome counters and bustling townsfolk already seated for breakfast.

Her chest tightened as she spotted him—Noah—moving behind the counter with that effortless ease she remembered so vividly. He rolled up his sleeves; his hair was slightly damp from his morning shower, and his eyes scanned orders with an intensity that always made her stomach flip.

I'm just here to help. That's all, she told herself, tightening the apron around her waist. *Nothing else.* Her pulse betrayed her calm. Just seeing him–hearing his voice–unravled the careful walls she had built around her heart. She was stronger than she used to be, but not invincible.

Noah's eyes caught hers, and his half-smile tugged at her resolve. "Emma," he called, voice carrying across the diner. "What are you doing here? Did you miss me, or are you just here to steal my secrets?"

Emma rolled her eyes but couldn't suppress a smile. "Maybe both," she said, moving closer. "You looked busy. Thought I'd lend a hand."

The morning passed in a blur of orders, spilled coffee, and shared laughter. Emma slid into the rhythm of the diner, prepping ingredients, helping with pastries, and exchanging playful jabs with Noah. Every brush of hands, every accidental touch sent warmth curling up her spine. Every glance made her pulse quicken. It was confusing–how could someone feel so familiar, so safe, and yet send her emotions into overdrive with just one look? She tried to remind herself of past lessons, but her heart refused to listen.

But then, as she reached for a tray of golden croissants, a quiet conversation caught her ear. Noah, whispering to a regular while Emma wiped a counter nearby, said:

"I don't know if I even belong here… Maplewood feels so small now. Maybe I'm just… not meant to stay."

She felt a constriction in her chest. Not meant to stay? Panic and confusion twisted together, a storm inside her chest. *He's leaving… again? After everything?* She wanted to step forward, to ask him if he meant it, to demand reassurance–but fear held her frozen. The memory of prior disappointments whispered louder than her desire to reach out.

Emma set the tray down slowly, forcing herself to take deep breaths. Her mind raced, visions of past heartbreak and late-night confessions flooding her thoughts. *I can't let myself get swept away again. I can't.*

Hazel, sitting at her usual corner booth, gave her a knowing glance. "Looks like someone just discovered their breakfast comes with a side of heartbreak," she teased. Emma tried to force a laugh, but it came out hollow. Hazel always knew more than she let on, and tonight, her friend's teasing cut through the pretenses Emma had been clinging to.

Emma groaned quietly, lowering her head. "Hazel… I don't know what to do," she admitted softly, stepping toward the corner booth. "I… I

can't keep letting him get close. Every time I did…
I ended up losing him. I can't do that again. "

Hazel arched a brow, amusement sparkling in her
eyes. "So… what? You're going to avoid him? Cold
shoulder him? Is that your master plan?"

Emma nodded, her jaw tightening. "I have to. I'm
going to keep my distance. Focus on the contest.
Focus on… myself. She repeated the words to
herself like a mantra, hoping that repetition would
harden her resolve. But every memory of Noah–the
brush of his hand, the warmth of his smile–slipped
past her mental defenses. I can't let my feelings get
in the way. Again. Noah doesn't care about me. He
got what he wanted and now he's going to leave
again, typically. You'd think I'd learned to stay
away from him."

Emma bit her lip, her gaze flitting toward Noah,
who was laughing with a customer behind the
counter, utterly unaware of the emotional storm
brewing inside her. *He does not know. He's
completely oblivious.* She envied his ease, his
ability to navigate the world without carrying the
weight of fear. If only she could unburden herself as
freely, but her heart refused to surrender.

With one last glance at him, she turned and left the
diner. The bell jingled softly behind her, but the

sound couldn't compete with the pounding of her own heart. Each step felt heavy, yet each memory of him pressed against her mind, a constant reminder of what she wanted but could not yet allow herself. The chilly autumn air did nothing to cool the fire inside. Outside, the crisp autumn air hit her face, carrying the scent of wet leaves and pumpkin spice—sweet, fleeting, and tinged with bittersweet longing.

Emma leaves the diner conflicted, tension simmering. Noah was unaware of her feelings.

As she walked home, she replayed every word, every glance, every accidental touch from the morning. *I must exercise caution. Protecting my heart is a must. I can't give in... again.* Her resolve stiffened with every step, an icy wall forming around her emotions. Yet even as she promised herself distance, she couldn't shake the warmth of Noah's touch or the memory of their stolen moments together. Her heart wavered, torn between caution and desire. She knew the contest would demand her focus, but the more she tried to lock him out, the stronger his presence became in her mind.

The contest was coming, and so was the chaos of emotions she had tried to contain. But Emma knew one thing for certain: she would have to keep her guard up, no matter how much her heart protested.

Chapter 24

Rivalry Rekindled

Maplewood's town hall had been transformed into a patchwork of autumnal splendor: garlands of golden leaves hung from the rafters, candles flickered on every table, and the smell of cinnamon, nutmeg, and baked apples made the air feel warm and inviting despite the crisp fall chill outside. The pie contest was in full swing, and the room buzzed with anticipation, laughter, and the occasional whispered gossip about past winners and local legends. Emma inhaled deeply, trying to absorb the warmth of the moment, but even the cozy scent of baked apples couldn't quiet the nervous flutter in her stomach. This was supposed to be her moment–a chance to prove she could stand on her own two feet, no matter who was watching.

Emma stepped in, heart hammering, her apron crisp and her rolling pin tucked under her arm like a shield. She had told herself she would remain focused, distant, professional—but the moment her eyes landed on Noah, standing at his station with calm ease, something inside her twisted. He looked relaxed, approachable, yet impossibly handsome in the soft glow of the hall's lights. It wasn't fair–how easily he could walk into a room and pull all the air with him. Emma's resolve wavered, and she had to grip the edge of her table just to steady herself. Focus, she reminded herself. Focus on the pie, not the man.

He caught her gaze briefly and smiled—just enough to make her stomach flutter—before returning to his work. Emma took a steadying breath and turned her attention to her station, arranging ingredients meticulously, trying not to let him see how much his presence affected her. The last she'd promised herself control, she'd ended up with flour on her face and his hands tangled in her hair. She couldn't afford that kind of distraction here–not when so much was on the line.

The first round began, and the tension in the room thickened like the rich custard she was about to bake. Contestants bustled, flour puffed into the air, and the judges whispered quietly, clipboard in hand. Emma worked with precision, each movement deliberate, each step a silent promise to herself: *Focus. No distractions. Stay away from him.* Her hands trembled slightly as she rolled the dough, not from nerves about the contest–but from the proximity of him. No matter how steady her movements looked, her heart was anything but.

Yet, even as she layered crust over fruit, she felt his eyes on her. Every glance, every fleeting smile, every subtle smirk reminded her of last night, of the storm, the flour fights, and the electricity that refused to die.

Noah's station wasn't far from hers, and she couldn't help noticing how effortlessly he moved—his hands shaping dough with care, his brow furrowed in concentration, the way he occasionally bit his lip as he tasted a filling. She remembered the first time she'd watched him bake–how every movement felt unhurried yet purposeful, like he was sculpting calm out of chaos. That same steadiness now only made her chest ache. Emma's resolve wavered, heat creeping up her neck, but she forced herself to concentrate.

The judging round arrived faster than she expected. Emma presented her pie, a perfect golden crust hiding the spicy-sweet pumpkin filling she had perfected over countless late nights. The judges nodded appreciatively, murmuring amongst themselves as they tasted each bite.

Noah stepped up next, his approach deceptively simple. He presented his pie with a quiet confidence, his flavors honest and nostalgic, reminding the judges of comfort and home. Emma blinked, impressed despite herself. *He's actually good,* she admitted internally. A reluctant smile tugged at her lips. Of course he was. He always surprised her in ways she didn't expect, just when she thought she had him figured out.

When the scores were announced, Emma's name rang out first—she had shined, her precision and bold flavors undeniable. Noah's pie received equally high marks, though his charm and simplicity seemed to steal the room in a different way. The crowd murmured, approving of both, their rivalry renewed but no longer bitter—electric, charged, and teasing.

As Emma packed up her ingredients, she felt Noah's gaze linger. He approached her station, a small, infuriating smile playing on his lips.

"You were amazing out there," he said softly, leaning close enough for her to feel the warmth radiating from him. His voice was too gentle, too sincere, and it disarmed her faster than any smirk ever could. For a heartbeat, she forgot about the contest, the people, everything but the warmth in his eyes.

Emma stiffened, brushing her hands over her apron. "Thanks. You... weren't bad yourself," she replied, keeping her tone neutral, hiding the flutter in her chest.

Noah chuckled low. "Just trying to keep up with you, Lawson. Don't want you thinking I've forgotten how to compete."

Emma's pulse jumped, and she took a step back, reminding herself of her promise to keep distance. "Well... I'm sure the judges appreciate simplicity as much as skill," she said, coolly.

He raised an eyebrow, stepping just slightly closer, his tone teasing. "You sound cold today. Something wrong, or are you just mad that I'm making this interesting for you?"

Emma froze for a heartbeat, then looked away, forcing a controlled smile. "No. Just... focused." Her throat tightened. She wanted to tell him that she wasn't cold–she was terrified. Terrified of falling again, of wanting him again. But all she managed was a faint smile and a quick nod.

Inside, though, her heart betrayed her, skipping and racing all at once. Every brush of his hand as he handed her a rolling pin, every accidental touch as they reached for sugar at the same time, made her pulse stutter. She could feel the tension simmering beneath her practiced coldness.

The round ended, the judges scribbling notes and announcing scores. Emma and Noah exchanged a glance—half-competitive, half-flirtatious—but the unspoken promise lingered in the air: *this rivalry was far from over.*

As the contestants cleaned up, Hazel's voice rang softly from across the room: "Watch yourself, Emma. He's going to be all over you before you know it." Hazel's words stung because they weren't entirely wrong. Every look from him felt like a promise, and Emma wasn't sure how many promises her heart could handle.

Emma froze, cheeks burning. "Hazel!" she whispered sharply, though her eyes betrayed a spark of acknowledgment. Hazel only smirked knowingly, leaving her to stew in the tension.

Noah caught her glance and gave a slow, knowing grin, leaning in just slightly before stepping back, maintaining the delicious torment between them. Emma forced herself to focus on her station, though her thoughts kept drifting—toward his hands, his smile, the way he looked at her…

The contest had begun, the rivalry was rekindled, and the stakes had never felt higher—both in the kitchen and in her heart and somewhere deep down, Emma knew this wasn't just about pies or ribbons anymore. It was about proving she could stand in front of him–not as the woman who loved him once, but as the one strong enough to choose what came next.

Chapter 25

Whipped Cream Confessions

The scent of vanilla and cinnamon lingered in Emma's kitchen, mingling with the crisp autumn air that drifted through the open window. Sunlight caught the rolling pins and bowls scattered across the counters, making the kitchen feel cozy, warm… and completely insufficient for the storm brewing inside Emma's chest. She had spent so many mornings in this kitchen chasing comfort in routine—sugar, butter, heat, and motion—but today, even the rhythm of baking couldn't soothe her. Every scent, every sound, reminded her of him.

Her mom, Linda Lawson, perched on a stool by the island, hands clasped over a cup of tea, eyes twinkling with that familiar mix of curiosity and expectation. "Emma," she began casually, "so… Noah Carter. He's back in town. How's that going for you? Still planning to ignore him, or is someone finally going to admit what they've been feeling?" Trust her mother to stir the one ingredient she'd been trying to leave out of her life lately.

Emma's hands stilled mid-whisk, and she felt her chest tighten. "Mom," she said carefully, trying to keep her tone neutral, "we're just… focusing on the contest. That's all." Even as she said it, the words tasted like a lie. She wasn't just focused on the contest—she was avoiding the look in his eyes that made her heart remember too much.

Linda raised an eyebrow, leaning forward slightly, the teasing edge in her voice unmistakable. "Focusing on the contest is one thing, sweetheart. But I know you. You've been carrying this crush since high school, and I see the way you look at him." Emma almost laughed—because it wasn't a crush anymore, not after everything they'd been through. It was something heavier, something that refused to fade no matter how hard she tried to bury it.

Emma's jaw clenched, heat rising in her cheeks. "Mom, please. I don't— I mean… it's not like that."

Linda sighed dramatically, but her eyes were warm, almost indulgent. "Emma, it's okay to like someone. You're not a child. You don't have to hide it forever. Life's too short to worry about pride or stupid rules you made for yourself."

Emma's hands trembled slightly, gripping her whisk tighter. The kitchen felt suddenly too small, too exposed, and her mother's words cut too close to the truth she had been trying to bury. "You don't understand," she burst out, voice rising. "You weren't there! You don't know what it's like to have someone leave and come back and expect everything to be perfect! You don't know what it's like to have your heart hanging on someone who may not even want it!" The words cracked open something she'd been holding in for years. The silence that followed wasn't awkward—it was raw, trembling, and full of all the heartbreak she had never said out loud.

Linda blinked, surprised, but didn't move. She gave a small, sympathetic nod. "Emma…" she said softly, but Emma wasn't done.

"I can't just… fall back into it like nothing happened! I can't pretend I'm not scared! And I'm not some… some girl who just waits around for a boy to make his mind up!" She threw her hands in the air, flour dusting her fingers like snow, the tension in her body spilling into the room.

Her mom's eyes softened, and she reached over, placing a comforting hand on Emma's. "You're not just a girl, Emma. You're smart, capable, and you deserve to fight for what you want… or protect yourself if you need to. But hiding? Avoiding? That won't make your heart any less tangled." Emma swallowed hard. Her mother always had a way of stripping the excuses down to truth. Maybe that's why baking was easier—you could follow the recipe, measure the outcome, control the heat. Feelings didn't work like that.

Emma bit her lip, exhaling slowly, feeling both guilty and relieved. She didn't look at her mother, instead focusing on the mixing bowl in front of her, as if the rhythmic motion of stirring could untangle her messy emotions.

Linda tilted her head, a teasing smile tugging at her lips. "And… between you and me?" she said quietly. "I think he's just as into you as you are into him. But someone's got to make the first move."

Emma froze mid-whisk, heat flaring in her chest. She could practically hear Noah's teasing voice in her head, the memory of his half-smile, the brush of his hand… *No. I can't.* And just like that, she wasn't in her kitchen anymore—she was back at the contest, watching his smile curve in that maddening way that made her forget every reason she had to stay guarded.

"I… I'm just… busy," Emma muttered, a weak attempt at deflection.

Linda laughed softly, shaking her head. "Busy, huh? Yeah, sure. Busy avoiding your feelings is one thing, but you're never going to win by hiding."

Emma's shoulders slumped, a small, defeated sigh escaping her lips. She knew her mother was right, and part of her hated that she had been caught, exposed by words she hadn't even wanted to admit aloud.

From somewhere in her memory, she felt the warmth of Noah's presence, the way he leaned close during the contest rounds, the tension that simmered between them like an unspoken promise. She shivered slightly, both from anticipation and guilt at avoiding him.

"Mom," she whispered finally, softer this time, "I just... I can't. Not yet. I need... space to figure this out."

Linda nodded, squeezing her hand gently. "I understand, pumpkin. But don't hide for too long. You might miss your chance." Emma's stomach twisted at the thought. Chances had a way of slipping through her fingers, especially the ones she wasn't brave enough to reach for.

Emma's gaze drifted to the bowl in front of her, then to the sunlight streaming across the counter.

Somewhere, deep down, she knew the contest wasn't the only challenge waiting for her. Her heart—and Noah—were part of the recipe now, and the heat was only getting higher. And for the first time, she wondered if she was ready to let herself burn.

Chapter 26

Piecing Together Hearts

The bakery smelled of cinnamon, vanilla, and freshly baked crusts, but the warmth of the ovens did nothing to ease the chill creeping up Emma's spine. She had been working since dawn, throwing herself into pastries and pie crusts, hoping that if her hands stayed busy, her heart wouldn't have time to remember the way his voice sounded when he said her name. She was kneading dough with the focus of a woman trying to avoid thinking about Noah—but the memory of him, of his intense eyes and teasing grin, refused to leave her mind.

The bell above the door chimed softly. Emma looked up, expecting a customer. Instead, she saw Noah standing there, casual as ever, leaning against the doorframe with that infuriating half-smile and a playful tilt to his head. Her pulse stuttered. Of course he would show up when she least expected him—Noah Carter never followed recipes, never waited for things to cool before diving in.

"Well, well," he drawled, voice low and teasing. "If it isn't the busiest baker in Maplewood. Busy, huh?"

Emma froze, hands on the dough. "I… I'm working," she said carefully, trying to keep her voice neutral. "You know… baking, the contest."

He strolled past her, unbothered by the flour dusting the countertops, and leaned against the prep table. "Ah, yes, the contest. I see how that goes. But I have to ask… you've been avoiding me this past week under the guise of being 'busy,' right?" It had been a week, maybe more, since they'd last spoken alone. Every day since the storm, she'd caught glimpses of him around town—at the diner, the market, the town square—but she'd turned the other way. It was easier than facing the ache that came with his smile.

Emma's chest tightened. Her pulse quickened, and for a second, she considered running. "I'm… I'm not avoiding you!" she shot back, though her voice wavered.

"Noah, please," she muttered, fingers gripping the dough, "don't do this."

"Do what?" he asked innocently, though the heat in his eyes betrayed him. "Point out the fact that you've been deliberately ignoring me? That you've barely looked at me unless absolutely necessary?"

Emma's jaw clenched, and she pulled the dough from the counter, kneading it with more force than necessary. "Because I can't just... throw myself at you like nothing ever happened! You left, Noah! You walked away, and I had to... I had to protect myself!" Her throat tightened at the memory—the morning he'd packed his truck, the way she'd stood on her porch pretending she didn't care. He hadn't even looked back.

Noah stepped closer, his expression softening but still intense. "Protect yourself? Emma, I wasn't thinking clearly when I left. I was burned out, scared... but it had nothing to do with you not being enough." His words were quiet, but they scraped at the wound she'd kept sealed for years. Apologies didn't change the empty months she'd spent wondering what she'd done wrong.

Emma's voice rose, the frustration pouring out. "It *felt* like it! And don't think I didn't hear what you said at the diner! You said you didn't know if you belonged here. That you weren't sure if Maplewood—or me—was something you should stay for!"

Noah froze, guilt flashing across his features. "Emma… that wasn't about you. That's not how I feel about you. I was scared, unsure… overwhelmed. I didn't know how to handle my own life, let alone us."

Emma's chest tightened, her eyes stinging. "It sounded like it was all about me. Like I wasn't enough. Like maybe you didn't want to stay with me at all." The confession slipped out before she could stop it. She hated how small her voice sounded—how much power his leaving still had over her.

He reached out, brushing a loose strand of flour-dusted hair from her face. "Emma, listen to me. You've always been more than enough. I left because I was running from myself, not from you. I regret every day I did. And now? I'm here. I want to stay. I want *us*—all of it. But I need you to trust me." Something in his tone made her chest ache. It wasn't the first time she'd heard a man say he was sorry, but it was the first time it felt like he meant it.

Her defenses wavered, but fear still rooted her in place. "And what if staying… ruins me? What if being with you messes up everything I've worked for?" The words came out sharper than she intended. She wasn't just afraid of him—she was afraid of losing herself again. Of falling so hard she'd forget the woman she'd worked to become while he was gone.

"Noah, I..." she trailed off, struggling to breathe, heart pounding.

"No," he interrupted softly, voice low and sincere, "you're not ruined, Emma. You're brilliant, strong, and capable. I'm not here to take that from you. I'm here to be part of it... part of you, if you'll let me."

She swallowed hard, heat rushing through her chest, fingers twitching toward him. "I... I don't know if I can..."

He leaned closer, just enough that she could feel the warmth radiating from him. "You can. Because I'm not going anywhere. And yes... I'll wait as long as you need... but it's going to be very hard." The sincerity in his voice was a dangerous thing—it made her want to believe him. And wanting was its own kind of risk.

Emma's chest tightened, heat rising at the nearness of him, but fear and doubt clenched her heart. "I... I don't know if I can..." she whispered, stepping back, her hands trembling.

His gaze softened, longing and frustration warring in his eyes. "I understand. I just... I need you to hear me. I'm not running this time. I want you. I want this—but I can't make you believe that yet."

Emma swallowed hard, conflicted. Every fiber of her wanted to reach for him, to give in, but the weight of the past week, the contest, and her own insecurities held her back. "I... I need time," she admitted reluctantly.

"Noah, I—" she stopped, voice cracking.

He nodded slowly, just enough to show he was listening, not pressuring. "Take all the time you need," he said, voice low and steady. "But I'm not going anywhere. I'll be here when you're ready." He meant it. She could see it in the stillness of his stance, the quiet patience that hadn't been there years ago. It was new... and it scared her even more than his charm ever did.

The space between them felt electric, every glance and brush of hands charged with longing—but the argument hadn't been fully resolved. Emma turned back to her dough, kneading furiously to hide the flustered racing of her heart. Noah lingered a moment longer, eyes soft yet intense, before stepping back toward the doorway, leaving the room simmering with unspoken words and unresolved desire. When the door finally closed behind him, the silence felt heavier than before. Emma pressed her hands into the dough, watching the flour bloom across her skin like dusted regret.

Time slowed, the air thick with unspoken promises. Two hearts still caught in a half-baked promise—close enough to feel the heat, but not ready to rise.

Chapter 27

The Taste of Forever

The morning sun filtered through the bakery windows, dust motes dancing lazily in the light. Emma Lawson sat at a corner table, her hands wrapped around a mug of coffee that had long gone cold. She hadn't slept well. Every time she closed her eyes, she saw his face—the hurt in his eyes, the way he'd said her name like it still meant something. It was easier to focus on the coffee, the quiet, the familiar smell of sugar and yeast that had always grounded her. She stared at the floor, tracing invisible lines with the tip of her finger, mind a whirlwind of confusion, desire, and stubborn pride. It had been a week since the argument in the bakery, and she'd replayed every word in her head. The look in his eyes when he'd said he wasn't running—that haunted her more than she wanted to admit. It was easier to stay angry than to risk believing him again.

Hazel slid into the seat across from her, the teasing spark in her eyes replaced by a rare seriousness.

"Emma," she began, voice firm, "you've been walking around with your walls up for a week. One week of ignoring Noah, avoiding him, pretending it's about baking… but we both know that's not the whole story." Hazel's words hit too close to home. Emma had always prided herself on control, on being the steady one, the one who didn't fall apart. But lately, that control felt like a mask slipping at the edges.Emma flinched. Hazel was right, as usual. She'd been using the contest as an excuse, burying herself in work so she wouldn't have to face the ache that came every time she thought of him.

Emma clenched her mug. "I… I don't know what to do, Hazel. He… he makes me feel things I can't control. And after what I overheard at the diner, I don't know if I can trust him. I just… I need space." Even as she said it, she knew space wasn't what she really needed. What she wanted was courage—enough to face him, to admit that his absence had carved something hollow inside her. Her voice cracked slightly. She hated how small she sounded, how easily Noah could unravel her composure with a single look. It reminded her too much of the girl she'd been before he left—the one who believed forever was promised.

Hazel shook her head, leaning forward. "Space isn't going to fix this. You're scared, yeah, but running

from someone who's showing up for you isn't
courage—it's hiding. And you're too smart, too
stubborn, and too damn passionate to let fear run the
show." Hazel had always been the fearless one—the
one who leapt before she looked. Emma envied that.
Because right now, every part of her was standing at
the edge of something real, and she couldn't move.
Hazel rarely used that tone with her—it was the
voice she saved for truths that hurt but needed to be
heard.

Emma's gaze fell to the table, guilt and longing
warring in her chest. "I know..." she whispered, but
the words felt empty even to her. She wanted to
argue, to defend her fear, but the words wouldn't
come. Because Hazel was right. She wasn't afraid
of Noah leaving again—she was afraid of what it
meant if he stayed.

"I know' isn't enough," Hazel said gently, placing a
hand over Emma's. "You have to decide if you're
willing to taste forever, Emma. Because he isn't
going anywhere, and he isn't asking you to jump
blindly—he's asking you to trust him. That's scary,
but it's also rare. And maybe... maybe it's worth
it."

Emma swallowed, the weight of Hazel's words
settling over her. She wanted to argue, to retreat, to

keep herself safe—but the truth burned hotter than her fear. As Hazel left to help a customer, Emma sat alone in the quiet hum of the bakery. Her coffee had gone cold, but her pulse hadn't slowed. She pressed her palm to her chest, whispering to the silence, "What if I let him in... and it's different this time?"

By the time Hazel left, Emma sat alone again, the echo of her friend's words buzzing louder than the clatter of dishes behind the counter. Somewhere across town, someone else was feeling the same pull—the same ache of wanting to fix what had been broken. Meanwhile across town Noah wiped his hands on a rag for the third time, the clatter of coffee cups and the murmur of regulars fading into background noise. He'd been at the diner since dawn, pretending that a busy morning rush could drown out the silence Emma left behind. It didn't work. He leaned against the counter, eyes distant, shoulders tense.

"Something's on your mind, Carter," said Joe, the diner cook, sliding a plate of pancakes toward him.

Noah shook his head, forcing a small, tired smile. "Yeah... I guess I've just been thinking a lot. About life. About staying here... about what I actually want for once, instead of running from it." He'd spent years chasing deadlines, new cities, and

Tanisha Pollard

empty victories. But none of it ever filled the quiet moments—the ones that used to belong to Emma. The thought of her laughter filling his mornings again was both terrifying and anchoring.

"Running?" asked Sarah, the waitress, curious.

He sighed, staring down at the syrup pooling on the plate. "I've been chasing things for so long... opportunities, work, success... everywhere but here. I thought moving, leaving, starting over somewhere else would fix me. But it never did. I just... I want roots. I want something that doesn't vanish when I turn my back." He thought about every late-night highway, every hotel room, every time he told himself that success would quiet the emptiness. It never did. Not until he saw her again.

Joe nodded, leaning on the counter. "Sounds like you're talking about more than the diner." Noah laughed softly, but there was no humor in it. The diner was just a symbol—proof that maybe, for once, he could belong somewhere that didn't demand he keep moving.

Noah chuckled, a little bitterly. "Yeah... more than the diner. It's Maplewood. It's everything I left behind. And it's her—Emma. She's... she's the one thing I didn't even realize I couldn't live without until I came back. And now I can't run anymore. I want to stay, to build, to… I don't know… be part of something lasting." He remembered that last night before he left—the argument, the way she wouldn't look at him. He thought leaving would make him stronger, more focused. Instead, it just made him lonelier.

Sarah smiled softly. "Sounds like you're ready for more than just a place. Sounds like you're ready for a life."

Noah ran a hand through his damp hair, eyes distant, voice low. "I just hope she'll let me in. That she'll believe me when I say I'm done running. I'm done escaping. I'm done hiding. I want her, and I want this—everything here. I just… I need her to trust me." He rubbed the back of his neck, the familiar ache of uncertainty pressing down on him. He wasn't good at waiting—but for her, he'd learn how.

Joe clapped him on the shoulder. "Then show her, son. Show her every day. Actions speak louder than words."

Noah nodded, a flicker of determination settling over his expression. "Yeah… I will. I'll make her see it. I'll make her see that staying isn't running. That loving her, building a life with her, that's exactly where I'm meant to be." For the first time in years, the idea of staying didn't feel like surrender—it felt like peace. And that scared him even more than leaving ever had.

Outside, the late autumn wind rattled the diner windows, carrying the scent of cinnamon and leaves through Maplewood's quiet streets. Somewhere across town, the same wind swept past the bakery, threading between two people trying to find the courage to stop hiding. Back at the bakery, Hazel's words still lingered in Emma's mind like a warm, dangerous spice. Her friend's voice mixed with the memory of Noah's—two truths tugging at opposite corners of her heart. She wanted to be brave, but bravery had always been easier in theory than in love. She traced circles on the table, thinking about the way Noah looked at her—steady, sure, like she was something worth staying for. It terrified her more than any contest ever could. She had always thought love was messy, unpredictable, something to be controlled or avoided. But Noah's persistence, his honesty, his presence—they made her question everything she thought she knew about herself.

She took a deep breath and whispered to herself, a promise, a dare, and a hope all wrapped into one: "I'm not running. Not this time."

Pumpkin Pie & Piercing Hearts

And across town, Noah whispered the same promise to the empty diner. Two hearts, beating in different kitchens, waiting for the right moment to rise.

The contest might decide who baked the better pie—but trust, love, and timing? Those were recipes still in progress.

Chapter 28

Heat You Can't Ignore

The late autumn sun cast long, golden slashes across the town square as the contest day reached its second round. Maplewood buzzed with excitement, the scent of baked goods mingling with crisp fall air, cinnamon, and the tang of apple. Booths were arranged along the street, each contestant showcasing their creations, and the crowd whispered eagerly about last week's surprises.

Emma adjusted her apron, taking a deep breath. Her hands trembled slightly, whether from nerves or anticipation, she couldn't tell. She smoothed the edge of her apron, the fabric soft against her palms, grounding her. The murmur of the crowd faded for a heartbeat, replaced by the steady rhythm of her own breath. This was her moment—a chance to prove she wasn't just the girl who'd been hurt, but the woman who'd built something from the ashes.

Across the square, her pies sat perfectly displayed, each crust golden, each filling rich with flavor and emotion. This contest wasn't just about winning—it was about proving she belonged here, proving to herself she could face the past and the people who had doubted her.

And then she saw him. Her pulse spiked, breath catching mid-inhale. It was like the air thinned just from his presence. The memories clawed their way back—his voice, the manipulation, the humiliation she'd sworn she'd buried.

Dean.

He sauntered past the crowd, that infuriating smirk glued to his face, eyes scanning the pies like a predator sizing up prey. Emma's stomach twisted, a mix of disgust and fear. She remembered too clearly the betrayal—the late-night heartbreak, the whispered lies, the way he had taken what wasn't his to take.

Dean leaned toward a bystander and whispered loudly enough for Emma to hear, "Hope your pies are as bland as the baker, Lawson. Wouldn't want anyone to actually enjoy them."

Emma's cheeks flamed, but she straightened her spine. She wasn't going to let him intimidate her today.

Noah, standing a few feet away by his own pies, noticed immediately. His jaw tightened, eyes narrowing with a protective intensity that sent a pulse straight to Emma's chest. Without hesitation, he strode toward Dean, the calm of his usual demeanor replaced with a dangerous edge.

"Excuse me," Noah said, voice low but carrying over the nearby chatter. Dean turned, expression shifting from smug to startled. "I think you need to leave." Emma's chest tightened as she watched him move—steady, certain, every line of his body radiating protectiveness. It wasn't about pride or ego. It was about her. And that realization hit harder than she expected.

Dean laughed, a sharp, arrogant sound. "Or what, Carter? You'll stop me?"

"I will," Noah said evenly, stepping closer, his presence solid and unyielding. "Emma doesn't need you bringing drama into her life. Not today, not ever."

The crowd started to murmur, sensing the tension. Emma's hands tightened around the edges of her display table, her pulse racing, but not from fear—she felt something new: the certainty that Noah had her back.

Dean sneered, leaning in slightly, his voice dripping with malice. "Always playing the hero, huh? Guess some things never change." For a moment, the entire square seemed to hold its breath. Even the autumn wind stilled, as if waiting to see whether Noah would swing or simply stand his ground.

Noah didn't flinch. "Not playing, Dean. Protecting. Something you've never understood."

Dean's smirk faltered as the crowd watched, the tension thick enough to cut with a knife. He took a slow step back, realizing he wasn't getting the upper hand today—not in front of the town, not against Noah.

Emma's breath caught, both from the adrenaline of seeing Noah stand up for her and the undeniable thrill coursing through her veins. The smell of cinnamon and baked apples seemed to mix with the electric heat radiating between them.

Dean, defeated in this public showdown, finally muttered, "This isn't over," and stalked off, vanishing into the bustling streets. Or so everyone thought.

A few minutes later, as the crowd's attention shifted toward the judges and the announcer's voice echoed across the square, Dean slipped back through the rows of tables. His smile was gone now—replaced by something colder, meaner. He paused by Emma's display, glancing around to make sure no one was watching.

With a flick of his wrist, he brushed one of the pie trays, just enough to loosen a delicate crust edge. A second nudge to the corner of her display table sent a thin crack spidering across the caramel glaze on her signature pie. It was quick, subtle—petty sabotage, invisible to anyone but a baker who knew perfection by heart.

By the time Emma turned back from talking to Hazel, Dean was gone again, swallowed by the crowd and the swirl of cinnamon-scented air. She frowned at her display—barely noticeable flaws, but she saw them. She always did.

Her heart stuttered. For a moment, the memory of his smirk threatened to unsteady her hands. But then she caught Noah's gaze across the square—steady, warm, unwavering—and the panic that had begun to rise… dissolved.

Not this time, she thought. *He doesn't get to win. Not even a little.*

Emma exhaled, a mixture of relief and lingering anger. Noah stepped close, lowering his voice so only she could hear. "You okay?" His eyes were soft, filled with something she couldn't quite name—pride, protection, longing. A week ago, she would've brushed him off, deflected with sarcasm. But something in her had shifted. Maybe it was the way he'd stood up for her without taking away her strength. Maybe it was finally realizing she didn't have to fight everything alone.

"I am now," she admitted, a smile tugging at the corners of her lips despite the residual tension.

He leaned a fraction closer, enough that she could feel the warmth of him, his subtle cologne mingling with the autumn air. "I meant what I said. Not just today. Not just in front of everyone. I've got your back, Emma. Always."

Her heart pounded, a mix of gratitude and a deeper, more urgent longing. She couldn't stop herself from brushing a loose strand of hair from her face. "I know," she whispered, voice thick with emotion.

Noah's lips twitched into a teasing, knowing smirk. "Good. Because I plan on making sure you feel that every day. In every way I can." The words shouldn't have made her blush like this—not here, not now—but they did. It wasn't just his voice, low and sincere—it was the promise threaded through it. And for the first time, she believed it.

The moment hung between them, charged with unspoken desire and trust, and Emma realized something she hadn't allowed herself to admit fully until now: she had never felt more seen, more protected, more alive.

The townspeople, oblivious to the private heat between them, cheered for other contestants, but Emma's attention was fully on Noah. Every glance, every brush of hands as he adjusted a pie display, every shared breath reminded her that she wasn't alone. Not in the contest, not in the town, and certainly not in the space between them.

As they returned to their respective stations to prep for the next round, Emma's hand brushed against Noah's, lingering a beat longer than necessary. The unspoken message was clear: they were in this together, and no sabotage—no matter how bitter—would break what was beginning to blossom between them. But as the judges approached and the crowd's energy swelled again, Emma realized this round was about more than pies. It was about courage—the kind that demanded she show up fully, for her craft and her heart.

Chapter 29

Gratitude and Goodbyes

The Maplewood town square was alive with energy, a swirl of autumn colors, laughter, and the unmistakable scent of freshly baked pies mingling with crisp fall air. Children darted between booths, leaves crunching under tiny boots, while the townsfolk buzzed with anticipation, their eyes darting from one pie display to another. Tables lined the streets, adorned with checkered cloths and small pumpkins, each contestant putting their heart and soul into their creations.

Emma Lawson adjusted her apron for the third time, fingers trembling slightly—not from nerves, but from the weight of expectation. She glanced at the pies in front of her, carefully lined and labeled, their golden crusts gleaming in the sunlight. This contest wasn't just about winning—it was about honoring her grandmother's legacy, proving that Maplewood hadn't forgotten the Lawson name, and showing herself that she was stronger than the timid girl who had once watched from the sidelines.

Just as she exhaled and took a step back from her table, a sudden commotion near the judges' tent caught her attention. Dean stood there, pretending to help one of the assistants arrange pie boxes. Her stomach dropped the moment she saw him lift one of hers—marked neatly with her name and the number she'd been assigned.

"Dean," she called, voice tight. "What are you doing?"

He froze, then flashed that too-smooth grin. "Just trying to help the judges set up. Thought I'd save them a trip."

Before she could reach him, the box in his hand slipped—or maybe it didn't. It tumbled to the ground, crashing open with a sickening splatter of caramel and crust. Gasps rippled through the crowd.

Emma's breath caught. Her best pie—the one she'd stayed up all night perfecting—lay in ruins at his feet. The sweet scent of caramelized sugar and apples suddenly turned bitter.

Noah was there in seconds, stepping protectively between them. "That was no accident," he said, his voice low and steady. "You've done enough, Dean."

Dean's jaw flexed. "You think you can waltz in here and take everything? The spotlight—her?"

"You didn't lose those things because of me," Noah said calmly. "You lost them because you couldn't stand that someone else might deserve them."

The murmurs of the crowd grew louder, spreading like wildfire through the square. Someone from the mayor's booth shouted for order, but Emma raised a trembling hand. "Let him go," she said quietly, her voice carrying more strength than she felt. "He's already lost."

Dean's smugness faltered. For the first time, he looked small—out of place in the town he'd once tried to control. With one last glare, he turned and stormed off, disappearing into the crowd.

The moment stretched in the silence he left behind. Emma exhaled shakily, her chest tight. Noah turned to her, eyes softening. "You've still got one pie left," he murmured, brushing her hand lightly. "And it's enough."

Her throat thickened, emotion rising like a tide. "Then I'll make it count," she whispered.

The judges moved systematically from booth to booth, tasting, nodding, whispering to one another.

Emma's remaining pie received murmurs of approval, subtle smiles, and nods, yet her gaze kept darting to Noah. She saw the slight tremor in his hand, the way his jaw tightened every time the judges stopped nearby. Her stomach dropped again.

He glanced up at her briefly, eyes soft but unreadable, and then—before she could react—he subtly sabotaged his own pie, lightly smearing the filling and adjusting the crust unevenly.

"Noah… what are you doing?" she whispered, taking cautious steps toward him.

He leaned close, lips barely moving as he mouthed, *For you.*

Her breath hitched. *For me?* The realization struck like a jolt—he must have seen what Dean had done. And Noah, in his quiet, infuriating way, was trying to even the playing field.

Emma's heart clenched. Fury, gratitude, and affection warred inside her. "I'm not letting you do this," she whispered fiercely. "I'll enter both pies. I can win on my own merit. Don't ruin yourself for me."

Noah's jaw flexed, but he nodded, eyes flicking to hers with deep admiration. "Then show me how fierce you can be, Lawson," he murmured, a teasing smile tugging at his lips.

For the first time, she saw past the charm—saw the man who believed in her when she didn't believe in herself. The noise of the crowd blurred, leaving only the warmth of his gaze steadying her.

As the judges continued, Emma's nerves coiled tighter. She watched every move, every tasting, every note the judges scribbled, each second stretching like an eternity. When they sampled her pie, subtle nods and quiet praise filled her with warmth—but still, worry lingered in the back of her mind for Noah.

Finally, the head judge stepped forward, clearing his throat. "And the winners of this year's Maplewood Thanksgiving Pie Contest..." The crowd leaned in, collective breaths held. "...are Emma Lawson and Noah Carter!"

A cheer erupted, a wave of applause and whistles washing over them. Emma's mouth fell open in disbelief. She glanced at Noah, whose grin was full of relief and pride, eyes sparkling with admiration for her. They had both won, yes—but together, as co-champions, and as something more.

Noah stepped closer, brushing a loose strand of hair from her face. "See?" he murmured, voice low and intimate. "You didn't need me to win. But I wouldn't let anyone take your moment either."

Emma's chest swelled, pride and gratitude mixing into a soft, dizzying joy. She reached up, fingers brushing his chest, feeling the steady heartbeat beneath his shirt. "You're impossible," she whispered, unable to hide the smile tugging at her lips.

"No," he countered, leaning in slightly, eyes glinting with warmth and mischief. "I'm devoted. And lucky. Very, very lucky."

Someone in the crowd shouted, "About time those two teamed up!" and laughter rippled through the square. The mayor wiped his eyes dramatically. "Maplewood's sweetest pair," he declared, and the crowd erupted again, their cheers wrapping around Emma like sunlight.

The townspeople's cheers faded into background noise as their private moment expanded, electric and tender. Every glance, every touch, every shared breath reminded Emma that she had never been more seen—or more protected—than she was in this moment.

Pumpkin Pie & Piercing Hearts

Hazel appeared beside them, a playful sparkle in her eyes. "I knew you two could do it," she said, nudging Emma's shoulder. "Now someone better make sure Carter doesn't get too full of himself before you celebrate properly."

Emma laughed softly, brushing flour from her hands, leaning against Noah's shoulder in a way she hadn't allowed herself to do all week. The warmth of his presence, the pride, the unspoken affection—it was intoxicating. For a fleeting moment, the world fell away, leaving only them, their victory, and the promise of something just beginning.

As the crowd dispersed, snapping photos and congratulating contestants, Emma caught Noah's eye and smirked. "Think you can keep up with me tonight?" she teased, a playful glint in her gaze.

"No," he said, voice husky, leaning closer so she could feel the heat radiating from him, "but I plan on trying."

As they walked toward the bakery, Emma glanced back at her table, at the pie Dean had tried to ruin. Instead, it gleamed under the fading sunlight—a reminder that even sabotage couldn't steal what she'd earned. For the first time, she didn't just feel proud. She felt free.

The promise lingered in the air as they walked back toward the bakery, hand brushing against hand, hearts full, and the autumn sunset painting Maplewood in shades of gold. Their victory was sweet, but the real triumph was something deeper—a connection forged through flour, fire, and the kind of trust and desire that could withstand any storm.

Chapter 30

Thanksgiving for Two

The sun dipped low behind Maplewood's rooftops, casting a golden glow across Emma's cozy home. The warm scent of roasting turkey, cinnamon, and freshly baked pies filled the kitchen, mixing with the laughter and chatter of her small but lively Thanksgiving gathering.

Her mom bustled around, tasting sauces, adjusting place settings, and offering gentle critiques. Hazel flitted between counters and chairs, ensuring drinks were topped up and everyone had a smile. Joe and Sasha were perched at the kitchen island, joking with Noah, who leaned casually against the counter, a small smudge of flour on his sleeve.

Emma moved between stations, adjusting a pie crust here, fluffing a napkin there. She stole a glance at Noah, who caught her eye with that infuriatingly charming smile. Her pulse quickened, but she told herself to focus—the dinner, the guests, the pies—not him. Her mind kept replaying the contest, the way he'd looked at her afterward—like she was more than the girl who baked her heart into pies.

That same look now sent warmth crawling up her neck.

"Emma, this looks perfect," her mom said, brushing a loose strand of hair from Emma's face. "I'm so proud of you… and you've really grown since your grandmother's day. I just hope someone special is noticing all this too." She raised an eyebrow pointedly.

Emma's cheeks warmed. She glanced at Noah, who was grinning at her from across the room. "He's not here to notice," she replied quickly, hiding her fluttering heartbeat.

Noah's smirk widened. "I hear that, Lawson," he called softly, leaning in closer as he passed. "But just so you know, I *always* notice."

Hazel, perched on a stool nearby, rolled her eyes with a knowing grin. "Oh, please. You two are ridiculous." Noah chuckled but there was something softer beneath it—a quiet affection that made her chest ache. He wasn't just teasing her anymore; he was learning her, piece by piece, like she was his favorite recipe.

The evening flowed with warmth and laughter. Plates were passed, stories shared, and pies were sampled with competitive bites and teasing comments. Every so often, Emma and Noah exchanged stolen glances, small touches as they reached for serving spoons, fingers brushing deliberately. Each time their fingers met, it lingered a little too long to be accidental. Every stolen glance felt like a secret promise neither of them was ready to say out loud.

The last of the dishes were being stacked in the sink, laughter and chatter winding down as the guests said their goodbyes. Emma's mom fussed over everyone, insisting they take leftovers home, while Joe and Sasha lingered to help tidy the kitchen. Hazel grabbed a few plates, teasing Emma about the "messy flour war" earlier.

Noah leaned against the counter, watching Emma with that familiar intensity that made her pulse race. She caught his gaze and felt a shiver run through her, the tension between them finally breaking free.

"You've been teasing me all evening," he murmured, stepping closer, voice low and playful. "Think it's about time we even the score."

Emma's breath hitched. "I… I don't know if that's a good idea," she whispered, but the flush creeping up her neck betrayed her words.

"Oh, I think it's a perfect idea," he said, tilting her chin up with one finger, brushing his thumb across her lips. The air between them shifted—thick with everything they hadn't said. The world outside quieted until all she could hear was the slow rhythm of his breathing and the distant crackle of the fire.

Hands brushed, lingering longer than necessary. His palm pressed against the small of her back, pulling her closer. Emma's hands found his chest, feeling the steady heartbeat that matched her own.

For once, she didn't hide behind her fear. She didn't question if she deserved this—him, them, this warmth. She simply let herself feel it.

The world outside—the Thanksgiving laughter, the cozy house full of friends and family—slipped away. All that mattered was the closeness, the laughter, and the long-awaited promise that had been building between them for months.

When they finally settled beside each other on the couch, the firelight painting soft gold across their skin, silence wasn't awkward—it was peace.

Emma pressed her forehead against Noah's chest. "Maybe... maybe this is what falling feels like," she whispered.

He tightened his hold on her, voice husky but
tender. "Yeah… maybe it is."

Outside, the last traces of daylight faded into night.
Inside, the scent of cinnamon lingered, warm and
familiar—a reminder that love, like baking, took
time, patience, and a little mess along the way.

The world beyond the walls of her home ceased to
exist. In that quiet, intimate cocoon, they let
themselves linger, letting love—sweet, messy, and
irresistible—finally have its way.

Epilogue 1

The Sweetest Yes

Snow fell softly outside the window of Emma's bakery, dusting Maplewood in shimmering white. Inside, the warmth of sugar and spice filled the air, mingling with the soft hum of laughter and holiday music. The bakery glowed with twinkle lights strung along the ceiling beams, reflecting off the glass cases filled with peppermint tarts, gingerbread cookies, and, of course, Emma's famous pumpkin pies.

It had been a year since that Thanksgiving night—the one that changed everything. Since then, the bakery and diner had merged into something even sweeter: *Sugar & Smoke*, the town's coziest café-bakery fusion, where locals came for comfort food, pie, and the unmistakable chemistry between its two owners.

Emma stood behind the counter, piping frosting onto a batch of cupcakes. A light dusting of powdered sugar clung to her hair, and a streak of chocolate smudged her cheek. Noah leaned against the doorframe, arms crossed, watching her with a lazy grin that never failed to make her blush.

Emma smiled faintly, brushing sugar off her sleeve. A year ago, she would've hidden behind the counter, terrified of attention. Now, laughter came easily—like warmth had finally settled into her bones. The bakery wasn't just hers anymore. It was theirs. And for the first time, she didn't feel like she had to prove she belonged.

"Careful," he drawled, "you're starting to look more like a dessert than what you're making."

She rolled her eyes, trying not to smile. "If you don't have something useful to say, Mr. Young, maybe you can help Hazel unpack the delivery."

From the front of the shop, Hazel's voice rang out, dry as ever. "Ha! Nice try. I'm on break. Watching you two flirt is more entertaining than any TV show I could stream."

Emma laughed, shaking her head. "You're terrible."

Hazel smirked. "Terribly invested, yes. You two owe me therapy bills for how long I had to watch your slow-burn disaster. I swear, it was like a horror movie that somehow turned into a rom-com." She pointed her coffee cup at Noah. "And if you *don't propose soon*, I'll kill you."

Noah grinned, playing it off. "Guess I'd better live dangerously then."

Hazel narrowed her eyes. "Try me."

Emma blushed, pretending to fuss with the cupcakes, but her heart was thudding wildly. She didn't notice Noah slipping behind the counter—until he was right behind her, his breath warm against her ear.

"You heard her," he murmured softly. "Guess it's time I stop stalling."

She froze, the frosting bag trembling in her hand. "Noah," she breathed, barely above a whisper, "what are you—"

He gently took her hand, turning her toward him. The bakery seemed to go still—the hum of the ovens, the faint chatter of customers—all fading into a soft hush. Hazel leaned against the counter, wide-eyed but grinning.

Her heart stumbled, the world narrowing to the soft scent of cinnamon and the sound of her own breath.

Pumpkin Pie & Piercing Hearts

Time seemed to still—like Maplewood itself was holding its breath.

Noah dropped to one knee.

Emma's breath caught. Powdered sugar drifted from her fingertips like snow.

He held out a small, velvet box—simple, elegant, and dusted with a bit of flour (because, of course, it was). Inside, nestled in cream satin, was a ring that sparkled with the softest firelight—an oval diamond framed by delicate leaf filigree, timeless and warm, just like her.

"Emma Lawson," he said, voice steady but thick with emotion. "You turned my world upside down and made me love every bit of it. You're the reason I stayed, the reason I smile, and the reason I believe in forever again. The first time you walked into that diner, you were all fire and flour," he said, smiling through his nerves. "And somehow, you managed to turn both into home."His smile turned crooked. "Will you marry me?"

Her hand flew to her mouth as tears filled her eyes. Hazel made a choked noise that might have been a sob—or a laugh.

Emma nodded, her voice trembling. "Yes. Yes, Noah. A thousand times yes."

The bakery erupted in applause—Hazel cheering the loudest, waving a piping bag like a victory flag. "Finally! My investment paid off!" she shouted.

Hazel whooped, her voice cracking, and someone shouted from the tables near the window—but Emma barely heard them. The only thing she could see was Noah, his eyes glassy, his hands steady as if the whole world had led to this one moment. Noah stood, sliding the ring onto Emma's trembling hand before pulling her in for a kiss that tasted like sugar, salt, and everything in between. The customers clapped, someone whistled, and Emma melted into him, laughing against his lips.

When they finally pulled apart, Hazel pretended to dab her eyes. "It's about time. I was *this close* to officiating your engagement out of sheer impatience."

Emma wiped at her tears, laughing. "You're impossible."

Hazel grinned, taking a sip of her coffee. "Oh, sweetheart, you'll thank me when I'm standing front and center at that wedding—preferably with cake privileges."

Pumpkin Pie & Piercing Hearts

Emma looked up at Noah, eyes gleaming. "Deal."

He smiled down at her, thumb brushing her ring finger. "Looks like we've got a lot of baking to do."

Hazel raised her cup. "To the next great recipe—love, chaos, and a whole lot of sugar."

Outside, the snow kept falling, blanketing Maplewood in quiet magic. Emma looked around her bakery—at the lights, the laughter, the life they'd built—and realized it wasn't just a happy ending. It was the beginning. A promise made of sugar and second chances.

Because love, like the perfect pie, was never about perfection—it was about getting your hands messy and tasting the sweetness anyway.

Epilogue 2

The Final Recipe

The autumn sun dipped low over Maplewood, washing the small community garden in molten gold. Trees framed the ceremony space like sentinels of color—burnt orange, honey, and crimson leaves dancing in the soft wind. Fairy lights were strung between the branches, twinkling like fireflies, and the faint hum of laughter floated through the crisp air. It felt fitting, Emma thought, that they'd chosen the same garden where everything began. A year ago, this place had been a tangle of overgrown weeds and unfinished dreams—now it bloomed with the same quiet determination she'd found in herself. The bakery had expanded, the town had rallied, and somehow, between the chaos and flour dust, she and Noah had built something that felt like home.

Emma stood at the edge of the aisle, her breath catching as she took it all in. Her dress was everything she'd never dared to dream of—soft ivory lace that hugged her curves before flowing into a light, airy skirt that shimmered with delicate embroidery of tiny leaves and vines, a nod to the season she loved most. The off-the-shoulder neckline framed her collarbones, where a simple gold chain rested—a locket that once belonged to her grandmother. Her hair was half up, loosely curled, dotted with small white blossoms that Hazel had insisted on weaving in that morning.

On her left hand gleamed a ring that caught the light like spun sugar—a vintage-inspired gold band with a small, oval diamond framed by two tiny leaves. It wasn't flashy, but it was *her*. The inscription inside, one she'd only seen this morning, read: *Home is wherever you are.*

Across the aisle, Noah stood beneath the wooden arch Hazel had built herself, lined with autumn leaves, baby's breath, and white pumpkins. He was almost too handsome in his black tux—no suspenders, no rustic flannel, just crisp lines and quiet confidence. His tie was the color of amber, and his hair was slightly tousled, like he'd run his fingers through it one too many times. His eyes found Emma's and held there, steady and sure, until she forgot how to breathe.

Hazel cleared her throat, trying to sound solemn but already grinning. "Okay, folks, settle down. I can't believe they actually let *me* officiate this thing, but here we are." Her grin softened for just a moment, her eyes shining. "You two made me believe in second chances again. That's saying a lot, considering I used to think happy endings were just for Hallmark movies." A ripple of laughter and awes went through the guests—friends, family, and the entire small-town circle that had watched this love story unfold like it was their favorite weekly show.

Hazel smirked. "I've had front-row seats to this romance from the beginning. And let me tell you, it started like a horror movie. So much denial. So much tension. I was ready to throw holy water at them." The crowd erupted. "But somewhere between flour fights, burnt pies, and emotionally charged baking sessions, these two idiots fell in love."

Emma laughed through the tears glistening in her eyes. Noah shook his head, smiling. Hazel turned soft now, voice lowering just enough to tug at every heart in the garden.

"They taught us that love isn't neat—it's messy, loud, sometimes sticky with caramel, but it's real. And that's what makes it beautiful. So, before I start crying harder than Emma's mom, let's make this official."

The guests chuckled as Hazel gestured for the rings. Joe passed them forward—two simple gold bands, hand-forged by a local artisan. Emma slipped Noah's ring onto his finger, her voice trembling with emotion.

"With you, I found peace I didn't know I needed... and chaos I didn't know I missed."

Noah smiled, his voice husky as he returned the gesture, sliding her ring into place. "You're my reason to stay. My favorite kind of forever."

Hazel sniffled, dramatically fanning her eyes. "Okay, I might cry now. By the power vested in me—thanks to the internet and poor judgment—I now pronounce you husband and wife. You may kiss the baker."

Noah didn't hesitate. He swept Emma into his arms and kissed her like he'd been waiting his whole life to taste her again. The crowd cheered, someone whistled, and Hazel raised her arms like she'd just scored a touchdown.

When they finally broke apart, breathless and laughing, Hazel called out, "If you two don't last forever, I swear I'll kill you!"

The guests roared with laughter, and Emma blushed, hiding her face in Noah's shoulder.

As twilight deepened, the reception glowed with lantern light and music. The dessert table overflowed—pumpkin pies, spiced tarts, and a towering wedding "pie cake" layered with whipped cream and caramel drizzle. Noah fed Emma a bite, smearing just enough cream on her lip to make her swat at him, laughter echoing beneath the stars.

Hazel clinked her glass, lifting it high. "To Emma and Noah—the proof that sometimes love takes the scenic route, but it always finds its way home. May your life be full of laughter, warmth, and just enough burnt crusts to keep things interesting."

Everyone toasted, the glasses clinking like tiny notes of music.

Later, when the garden had quieted and the guests had gone, Noah took Emma's hand, his thumb brushing the ring that now gleamed on her finger. "Still think I don't notice?" he murmured.

She smiled, eyes soft and full. "I'd say you notice everything that matters."

In the distance, the bakery sign still glowed faintly against the night—*Sugar & Smoke* the name they'd all chosen together. Tomorrow, Emma knew they'd be back there, sleeves rolled up, laughter spilling between batches of pie crust and caramel drizzle.

Married or not, life would go on the same way it always had—sweet, messy, and entirely theirs. The leaves rustled softly overhead as he pulled her close for another kiss, slow and deep—the kind that spoke of forever.

Emma's Kitchen — A Taste of Love and Home

Recipes inspired by **Pumpkin Pie and Piercing Hearts** *(by Chef Tanisha)*

Food is memory. It's love. It's the way Emma learned to speak when words were too fragile — and the way Noah finally learned to listen. Every pie crust, every sprinkle of cinnamon, every late-night kitchen confession meant something more.

These are the recipes that filled her kitchen, and maybe... her heart.
From my kitchen to yours — may you find love in the mess, peace in the baking, and warmth in every bite.

Emma's Signature Pumpkin Pie

The heart of the story — and the one that started it all.
A flaky, buttery crust filled with silky pumpkin custard, warm spices, and a drizzle of caramel that makes hearts melt faster than Noah's smirk.

Homemade Pie Crust:

- *2 ½ cups all-purpose flour*

- *1 teaspoon salt*

- *1 tablespoon sugar*

- *1 cup (2 sticks) cold unsalted butter, cubed*

- *6 tablespoons ice water*

Instructions:

1. *In a large bowl, whisk together flour, salt, and sugar.*

2. *Cut in cold butter until the texture looks like coarse crumbs.*

3. *Add ice water one tablespoon at a time until the dough holds together.*

4. *Shape into a disk, wrap, and chill for at least 1 hour.*

5. *Roll out and fit into a 9-inch pie dish. Chill again for 15 minutes.*

Pumpkin Filling:

- *1 ½ cups pumpkin purée (homemade or canned)*

- *¾ cup brown sugar*

- *2 large eggs + 1 yolk*

- *1 ¼ cups heavy cream*

- *1 teaspoon vanilla extract*

- *1 teaspoon ground cinnamon*

Pumpkin Pie & Piercing Hearts

- ½ teaspoon ground ginger

- ¼ teaspoon ground nutmeg

- Pinch of salt

Instructions:

1. Preheat the oven to 375°F (190°C).

2. Whisk together all ingredients until smooth.

3. Pour filling into the prepared crust and bake for 45–50 minutes, or until the center is just set.

4. Cool completely before serving.

5. Optional: drizzle with homemade caramel or serve with the whipped cream that changed everything.

Tanisha Pollard

Hazel's Spiked Apple Cider

*For when the heart needs warming and the
company is too good to leave.
Hints of clove, orange peel, and cinnamon — best
served in mismatched mugs over gossip and
laughter.*

Ingredients:

- *1 gallon fresh apple cider*

- *1 orange, sliced*

- *4 cinnamon sticks*

- *6 whole cloves*

- *1-inch piece of fresh ginger, sliced*

- *¼ cup brown sugar (adjust to taste)*

- *½ cup bourbon or dark rum (optional)*

Instructions:

Pumpkin Pie & Piercing Hearts

1. *In a large pot, combine cider, orange slices, spices, ginger, and sugar.*

2. *Simmer over low heat for 30–40 minutes — do not boil.*

3. *Strain and stir in bourbon or rum if desired.*

4. *Serve hot, garnished with a cinnamon stick or orange twist.*

Tanisha Pollard

Late-Night Chocolate Chunk Cookies

*The batch that turned from "just baking" into
something more.
Thick, gooey, and messy — just like falling in love
when you swore you wouldn't.*

Ingredients:

- *1 cup unsalted butter, melted and slightly
  cooled*

- *1 cup brown sugar*

- *½ cup granulated sugar*

- *2 large eggs*

- *2 teaspoons vanilla extract*

- *2 ¾ cups all-purpose flour*

- *1 teaspoon baking soda*

- *½ teaspoon salt*

- *2 cups dark chocolate chunks*

- *Flaky sea salt (for topping)*

Instructions:

1. *Preheat the oven to 350°F (175°C). Line baking sheets with parchment.*

2. *In a large bowl, whisk melted butter, brown sugar, and granulated sugar until smooth.*

3. *Add eggs and vanilla; whisk until glossy.*

4. *Stir in flour, baking soda, and salt until just combined.*

5. *Fold in chocolate chunks.*

6. *Scoop dough onto trays, chill for 10 minutes, then bake 10–12 minutes until golden at the edges and soft in the center.*

7. *Sprinkle with flaky salt while warm.*

Maple Pecan Bars

*A family favorite that survived the chaos of
Thanksgiving dinner.*
 *Crunchy pecan topping, caramel filling, and
buttery shortbread — perfect for awkward family
gatherings or making peace after a fight.*

Crust:

- *2 cups all-purpose flour*

- *½ cup powdered sugar*

- *1 cup cold butter, cubed*

Topping:

- *¾ cup brown sugar*

- *½ cup pure maple syrup*

- *⅓ cup heavy cream*

- *2 tablespoons butter*

- *2 cups chopped pecans*

Pumpkin Pie & Piercing Hearts

Instructions:

1. Preheat the oven to 350°F (175°C).

2. Combine crust ingredients and press into a parchment-lined 9x13 pan. Bake for 15 minutes.

3. In a saucepan, combine brown sugar, maple syrup, butter, and cream. Bring to a simmer for 2 minutes.

4. Stir in pecans, then pour mixture over the warm crust.

5. Bake for another 20–25 minutes until bubbling and golden.

6. Cool completely before slicing into squares.

Tanisha Pollard

Hazel's "Don't Fall for Him" Latte

Spoiler: she did anyway.
Espresso, cinnamon, and a swirl of vanilla cream
— sip when your heart's confused but hopeful.

Ingredients:

- *1 shot of espresso (or ½ cup strong coffee)*

- *¾ cup steamed milk*

- *1 tablespoon vanilla syrup*

- *Pinch of cinnamon*

- *Whipped cream (recipe below)*

Instructions:

1. *Pour espresso into your favorite mug.*

2. *Stir in vanilla syrup and sprinkle cinnamon.*

3. *Top with steamed milk and a generous swirl of homemade whipped cream.*

Homemade Whipped Cream (The Kiss That Started It All)

This is the one that started it — the moment sugar, laughter, and tension turned into something much sweeter.

Ingredients:

- *1 cup heavy whipping cream, chilled*

- *2 tablespoons powdered sugar*

- *1 teaspoon pure vanilla extract*

Instructions:

1. *Chill your mixing bowl and beaters for 10 minutes.*

2. *Pour in cold cream and beat on medium until it thickens.*

3. *Add powdered sugar and vanilla; increase speed to high.*

4. *Whip until soft peaks form — luxurious, silky, and ready to dollop over pie... or someone's smirk.*

Emma's Caramel Sauce

*Golden, glossy, and addictive — much like the
chemistry that started in her kitchen.*

Ingredients:

- *1 cup granulated sugar*

- *6 tbsp unsalted butter, cubed*

- *½ cup heavy cream (room temperature)*

- *1 tsp vanilla extract*

- *Pinch of sea salt*

Instructions:

1. *In a heavy saucepan over medium heat, melt
   sugar slowly, stirring occasionally, until
   amber and smooth.*

2. *Add butter carefully — it will bubble. Stir
   until melted.*

3. *Slowly pour in cream while whisking constantly.*

4. *Remove from heat, stir in vanilla and salt.*

5. *Cool slightly before drizzling over pie, coffee, or someone you shouldn't be falling for.*

Noah's Diner Classic: Buttermilk Pancakes with Cinnamon Butter

*The kind of breakfast that made his diner famous —
warm, indulgent, and made for sharing on lazy
mornings when love feels like home.*

Pancakes:

- *2 cups all-purpose flour*

- *2 tbsp sugar*

- *2 tsp baking powder*

- *1 tsp baking soda*

- *½ tsp salt*

- *2 cups buttermilk*

- *2 large eggs*

- *¼ cup melted butter*

257

- *1 tsp vanilla extract*

Cinnamon Butter:

- *½ cup unsalted butter, softened*

- *2 tbsp honey*

- *1 tsp cinnamon*

- *Pinch of salt*

Instructions:

1. *Whisk flour, sugar, baking powder, baking soda, and salt in a bowl.*

2. *In another, combine buttermilk, eggs, butter, and vanilla.*

3. *Pour wet into dry, stir until just combined — a few lumps are fine.*

4. *Cook on a buttered skillet over medium heat until golden.*

5. *Mix cinnamon butter ingredients and serve over warm pancakes, letting it melt into every crevice like a promise that sticks.*

Tanisha Pollard

"Second Chances" Brown Butter Blondies

Rich, golden, and impossible to forget — just like the one that got away but somehow found his way back.

Ingredients:

- *1 cup unsalted butter*

- *1 ½ cups brown sugar*

- *2 large eggs*

- *2 tsp vanilla extract*

- *2 cups all-purpose flour*

- *½ tsp baking powder*

- *½ tsp salt*

- *½ cup white chocolate chips*

- *½ cup chopped pecans (optional)*

Instructions:

1. *Preheat the oven to 350°F (175°C). Line an 8x8 pan with parchment paper.*

2. *Melt butter in a saucepan over medium heat until it turns golden brown and smells nutty. Let cool slightly.*

3. *Whisk in brown sugar, eggs, and vanilla.*

4. *Fold in flour, baking powder, and salt.*

5. *Stir in chocolate chips and pecans if using.*

6. *Spread batter into the pan and bake for 25–30 minutes, until edges are set but the center is soft.*

7. *Cool before slicing — or don't. Some things are meant to be messy.*

Tanisha Pollard

Emma & Noah's

Midnight Strawberry

Cobbler

Sweet, messy, and made under a blanket of stars.

The kind of dessert that starts as a late-night

craving and ends as a confession neither of them

planned.

Ingredients:

4 cups fresh strawberries, hulled and halved

½ cup granulated sugar

1 tbsp cornstarch

1 tsp lemon juice

1 cup all-purpose flour

2 tbsp sugar

1 ½ tsp baking powder

¼ tsp salt

½ cup cold butter, cubed

⅓ cup milk

1 tsp vanilla extract

Instructions:

1. *Preheat the oven to 375°F (190°C).*

2. *In a bowl, toss strawberries with sugar, cornstarch, and lemon juice. Pour into a greased baking dish.*

3. *In another bowl, mix flour, sugar, baking powder, and salt.*

4. *Cut in butter until crumbly, then stir in milk and vanilla until just combined.*

5. *Drop spoonfuls of dough over strawberries.*

6. *Bake for 30–35 minutes until golden and bubbling.*

7. *Serve warm with a scoop of vanilla ice cream — or share straight from the dish when words fall short.*

Cozy Cabin Hot Cocoa

For snowed-in nights, honest talks, and the kind of warmth that doesn't come from the fire.

Rich, velvety, and topped with a cloud of whipped cream — a reminder that love, like cocoa, is best when shared.

Ingredients:

- *2 cups whole milk*

- *½ cup heavy cream*

- *2 tablespoons unsweetened cocoa powder*

- *2 tablespoons granulated sugar*

- *¼ cup semisweet chocolate chips or chopped chocolate*

- *½ teaspoon vanilla extract*

- *Pinch of salt*

Instructions:

1. *In a small saucepan, whisk together milk, cream, cocoa powder, and sugar over medium heat until steaming.*

2. *Add chocolate chips and stir until melted and smooth.*

3. *Remove from heat and whisk in vanilla and salt.*

4. *Pour into mugs and top with whipped cream or marshmallows.*

5. *Optional: add a dash of cinnamon or peppermint — or share a sip with someone who makes the cold fade away.*

Tanisha Pollard

Acknowledgements

To everyone who's ever found healing in the kitchen

— this story is for you.

To my dad, Andy Pollard, who taught me that food

is love even when words fall short. To my friends

and family who taste-tested my late-night bakes and

never complained (too much) about the mess.

Pumpkin Pie & Piercing Hearts

To the readers who believed in Emma and Noah —

thank you for letting me share a love story that isn't

perfect but is full of flavor, forgiveness, and second

chances. You've made this world of flour, sugar, and

heartache come alive.

To every woman who's ever doubted her strength,

her worth, or her dreams: keep mixing, keep rising.

You are more than enough — messy dough, broken

crust, and all.

And finally, to every baker, dreamer, and romantic

out there — may your life always smell faintly of

cinnamon and courage.

Tanisha Pollard

Author's Note: A Taste

That Lasts

When I started writing Pumpkin Pie and Piercing

Hearts, I wanted to tell a story that felt like coming

home — warm, complicated, a little bit sticky, and

full of love you can taste.

Emma's journey taught me that sometimes the

bravest thing you can do is stay — in your kitchen,

in your feelings, in the messy, beautiful middle of

becoming who you are. Noah reminded me that love

doesn't have to be grand to be real — it just has to

show up, every day, even when it's hard.

Pumpkin Pie & Piercing Hearts

If this story made you laugh, ache, crave pie, or

believe in love a little more... then it's done its job.

Thank you for reading, for baking, for feeling every

word.

May your love be as warm as your pie, your

healing as sweet as your caramel sauce,

and your endings — always — taste like home.

About the Author

Tanisha Pollard was born and raised in Antigua and Barbuda in the Caribbean before moving to New York at age twelve and eventually settling in Georgia. A lifelong storyteller and devoted romance reader, she finally decided to stop doubting herself and began writing the love stories she had always dreamed of sharing with the world.

Alongside her writing, Tanisha works as a patient care technician while pursuing a career in radiology. She is also a trained chef and former Disney cook, blending creativity and passion into every part of her life. As a woman living with PCOS, Tanisha hopes her stories inspire readers to embrace their own journeys, take bold chances, and believe in their worth.

When she isn't writing, Tanisha can be found reading stacks of romance novels, experimenting in the kitchen, or dreaming up her next happily ever after.